LAST PICK

David Starr

James Lorimer & Company Ltd., Publishers
Toronto

James Lorimer & Company Ltd., Publishers acknowledges funding support from
the Ontario Arts Council (OAC), an agency of the Government of Ontario.
We acknowledge the support of the Canada Council for the Arts, which
last year invested $153 million to bring the arts to Canadians throughout the
country. This project has been made possible in part by the Government of
Canada and with the support of Ontario Creates.

Cover design: Tyler Cleroux
Cover image: Shutterstock

9781459415829
eBook also available 9781459415812

Cataloguing data for the hardcover edition is available from Library and
Archives Canada.

Library and Archives Canada Cataloguing in Publication (Paperback)

Title: Last pick / David Starr.
Names: Starr, David (School principal), author.
Series: Sports stories.
Description: Series statement: Sports stories
Identifiers: Canadiana (print) 20200357166 | Canadiana (ebook) 20200357190
| ISBN 9781459415805 (softcover) | ISBN 9781459415812 (EPUB)
Classification: LCC PS8637.T365 L37 2021 | DDC jC813/.6—dc23

Published by:
James Lorimer &
Company Ltd., Publishers
117 Peter Street, Suite 304
Toronto, ON, Canada
M5V 0M3
www.lorimer.ca

Distributed in Canada by:
Formac Lorimer Books
5502 Atlantic Street
Halifax, NS, Canada
B3H 1G4

Distributed in the US by:
Lerner Publisher Services
241 1st Ave. N.
Minneapolis, MN, USA
55401
www.lernerbooks.com

Printed and bound in Canada.
Manufactured by Friesens in Altona, MB in January 2021.
Job #272124

This book is dedicated to Karin Khuong.
2K Strong.

Contents

Prologue
THE BATTLE OF THE BIRDS

The Pacific Event Centre was full. Thousands of fans chanted loudly, waved flags and held up signs with the names of their teams. The atmosphere was electric. Thirteen-year-old Jaspreet "Jazz" Sidhu was more excited than she'd ever been in her life. Below, on the hardwood floor, her older sister, Akisha, and the rest of the Northside Ravens senior girls' basketball team were playing the Kelowna Falcons for the provincial championship. The game had been nicknamed "the battle of the birds." The Northside Ravens were the clear underdogs. Kelowna was looking to repeat as the champions.

Jazz sat with her mom and her best friend, Karin Santos. They were in the middle of a large crowd of Northside fans, all dressed up in red and black, cheering loudly — though none as loud as Jazz.

Northside Secondary, a sports powerhouse from suburban Vancouver, had won many provincial championships on the boys' side. Today was the girls' turn.

But things weren't looking good for the Ravens. Not good at all.

The Ravens had just scored, but were still down by one point with ten seconds left in the game. The score was 61–60 Kelowna. Across the arena, hundreds of Kelowna Falcons fans were smiling, yelling and high-fiving each other. Kelowna had the ball; all they had to do was inbound and hold onto it, and they would win.

Before the Kelowna player tried to inbound the ball, her coach called a time out. Both teams hurried to their benches and huddled around their coaches. Ms. Yao, the Ravens coach, picked up her clipboard and drew madly.

"Smart move by the Kelowna coach," said Karin.

Jazz groaned. Kelowna was still up by one, and now they could inbound the ball at half court. Things had looked bad for the Ravens. Now they seemed impossible.

The horn sounded. The teams broke their huddles and hurried onto the court. The referee gave the ball to a Kelowna player on the sidelines, then blew her whistle. The Kelowna fans hooted and cheered as if they already had the title. Jazz held her breath and hoped for a miracle.

Akisha was covering the girl trying to inbound the ball. She jumped up and down, waving her hands, preventing a clear pass. One second, two seconds, three seconds. The Falcons were out of time outs, and if Kelowna couldn't get the ball in play within five seconds, they would have to turn it over and give the Ravens one last chance.

Suddenly, the inbounding player head faked to the left. She tossed the ball to the right, where a teammate was open. Jazz watched as Akisha leaped up as high as she could. Akisha's fingertips touched the ball and changed its direction. The ball dropped to the floor. The clock started. Ten seconds, nine seconds, eight seconds.

Jazz could hardly watch as Akisha turned on her heels and picked up the loose ball. In one smooth motion, Akisha sprinted down the court to the Falcons' basket. Seven, six, five, four. The entire Kelowna team ran desperately after her. Three seconds.

"Shoot, Akisha!" Jazz shouted as her sister reached the top of the key. The fastest Kelowna girl was just steps away and gaining.

Two seconds. Akisha went in for a layup. Jazz watched, her heart pounding so loud it sounded like thunder in her chest. One second. The ball left Akisha's right hand. The horn sounded as the ball rose into the air. The ball gently touched the glass backboard in the middle of the black square, then fell cleanly through the hoop.

It took a second or two for most of the fans to understand what had just happened. But Jazz knew right away. The ball was in the air before the horn sounded. The shot was good. The Ravens had won by a single point.

The Kelowna team knew what happened as well. Some dropped to their knees in disbelief. Some cried. Others just stood, frozen in place. Their fans on the other side of the arena, so loud and confident just seconds before, fell into a shocked silence. But not the Ravens' supporters. The proof was on the game clock — 62–61 Ravens. All around Jazz, Ravens fans stood up, hugged each other and cheered. The Northside Ravens senior girls had won the most important game in the team's history. And Akisha Sidhu, Jazz's sister, had scored the winning basket.

"Five years from now," Karin said, "that could be us winning the provincial championship."

"Maybe," Jazz replied. But inside she knew she would never play on a championship team — or any team at all.

1 I'm Not MY SISTER

"Great shot, Jazz! Nothing but net! Nice to see you, too, Karin."

Jazz smiled at the woman walking her dog past the house. It had been a good shot. Jazz had taken a pass from Karin and released the ball out from where the three-point line would have been.

"Thanks, Ms. Yao." Ms. Yao was a counsellor at Northside Secondary School, the school Jazz would start next week as a Grade Eight student. Jazz had known Ms. Yao for ages. Ms. Yao was also the senior girls' basketball coach and had coached Jazz's older sister, Akisha, the spring before. That was when the Ravens won the provincial championship.

Akisha was playing for the Varsity Blues, as she had earned academic and athletic scholarships to the University of Toronto. Akisha had flown to Toronto a week before and Jazz really missed her. Toronto was a long way from Vancouver. With just Jazz and her mom left, the house seemed empty.

"Akisha sure had a great season last year," said Ms. Yao.

Jazz put down the ball and petted Ms. Yao's dog, a golden retriever called Magic. Magic wagged his tail happily. He was named after the famous basketball player Magic Johnson. Jazz had known him since he was a puppy.

"I wouldn't be surprised if your sister made the national team as well," said Ms. Yao. "Akisha isn't the most naturally talented player I've coached, but she sure is the hardest worker. I hope you girls play next year. I watched you both as I walked down the street. You look pretty sharp."

"Don't worry, Ms. Yao," Karin said. "I'm trying out for sure."

"What about you, Jazz?" asked Ms. Yao. "I'd love to coach another Sidhu."

"Thanks, Ms. Yao," said Jazz. "Maybe I will."

"Come on, Magic," Ms. Yao said to the dog. "It's time to carry on with your walk." Magic was sitting on the driveway and didn't seem very interested in walking. "Get moving, dog. I don't want you to get spoiled from all the attention." Magic finally got to his feet. "See you next week, girls. Jazz, the ball season doesn't start for two months, but I really hope you think about playing."

"I should go, too, Jazz," said Karin. "Mom wants to take me back-to-school shopping. We start high school in five days. Can you believe it? How are you feeling, Jazz?"

"I'm a bit nervous but okay," said Jazz. "Talk later?"

Karin said she'd message Jazz for sure, then walked down the street towards her home. Jazz was about to start shooting the ball again when her mother stepped out of the house.

"Ms. Yao's right, you know. You should try out. If your sister can do it, why can't you?"

Jazz cringed. Here we go again, she thought. She was getting very tired of this conversation. "Because I'm not Akisha, Mom. I'm not going to get scholarships and I'm not going to play for the school team."

"Why not, Jazz? Because of your condition? You learned all sorts of strategies when you were in therapy. You're no different from any other kid, now. Look at you on the court, sinking shot after shot."

Jazz struggled to hold back her temper. In kindergarten, Jazz had been diagnosed with Developmental Coordination Disorder. The condition affected her coordination and her ability to do things other kids found to be easy. Jazz had spent a lot of time in occupational and speech therapy when she was in elementary school. Therapy made Jazz feel awkward and stupid and different. She had hated every minute of it, even though it worked.

"I don't want to talk about this right now, Mom."

Last Pick

"You never do," said her mom. "Your problem isn't DCD, Jaspreet. It's attitude. Terry Fox lost a leg to cancer and look what he did. Rick Hansen couldn't walk but he travelled around the world. All I'm saying is if those people didn't let their disabilities get in the way of their dreams, why should you? I know you love basketball."

Jazz was getting angry. "Did Terry Fox have to go to speech therapy because he couldn't talk without stuttering? Did Rick Hansen get teased in PE class because he couldn't catch a ball or use scissors properly? No, Mom, they didn't. But I did! Last Pick, remember? I was the last kid chosen every time we played games. It happened so much that it became my nickname. That was all thanks to Mia Hanson and those terrible posts and memes she made up about me. Not to mention the face-to-face bullying. Last Pick. How would you like that name? Even with therapy, I still sometimes feel like I have two left feet and a brain that doesn't work properly."

"Jazz, listen to me. That online thing with Mia was more than two years ago. And she got in trouble for that and had to move schools. Forget about her. You have come so far. Leave the past in the past. Listen to the little voice inside your head. It will tell you to do the right thing."

Leave your past in the past. The little voice inside your head. Jazz's mom read a lot of self-help books.

As much as Jazz loved her mom, the sayings she picked up from the books drove her crazy.

"Do you remember the last time I played on a sports team?" asked Jazz. "Grade four? You signed me up for Metro Soccer? I was the only kid on the team to not get a single goal all season. Nobody would pass to me. Nobody invited me to birthday parties and playdates. Nobody even wanted to talk to me."

"Jazz, I know it was hard for you. But you have to believe in yourself. Take one day at a time."

"Believe in myself?" said Jazz. "Take one day at a time? Are you kidding me, Mom? The other kids treated me like I was some sort of freak. I stuck it out for the season like you said I had to, but I told you I would never go through that again. I'm done being last pick. The little voice inside my head is telling me I'm not my sister. And it's saying that I'm not going to play. So don't ever ask me again."

2 The First DAY

When her first day in grade eight arrived, Jazz had forgotten all about the argument with her mom. The Tuesday after Labour Day was beautiful and sunny as Jazz walked to Northside with Karin. They were still very nervous. When they left school in June, Jazz and Karin had been in grade seven, the oldest kids. Now they were the youngest in a school of more than sixteen hundred students.

"I don't know why you're worried, Jazz," said Karin when they reached the school. "You pretty much grew up here watching Akisha play."

"I know the gym," Jazz replied as they stepped into the building. "But that's about it. I sure don't know where we have to go for homeroom. The email said we were to find our homeroom class, get our schedules and then go on a tour of the school. But how are we supposed to do any of that?"

"You ask us and we'll help you." The girl speaking had long brown curly hair and was wearing a black-and-red Northside T-shirt. "My name's Franca," she said. "I'm one of the LINK Leaders at Northside. LINK stands for leadership, integrity and kindness, the school's three pillars. Our job is to help new students like you find their way around the school."

"I know LINK," Jazz said. "My sister was a LINK Leader. Her name is Akisha Sidhu. She graduated last year."

"Akisha's your sister?" said another LINK Leader, a short boy with glasses. "I know Akisha. She's great! I'm Richie and here are Trista, Rosie and Johnny." He introduced three more LINK Leaders in the same T-shirts.

"The homeroom lists are posted on the wall at the other end of the Commons," Rosie said. The Commons was the central atrium of the school. It served as the cafeteria as well as a meeting place for the students. There were hundreds of kids milling around, standing in small groups or sitting at the long tables.

"You could fight your way through the Commons," said Rosie. "Or I could pull up the list on my phone and tell you where you are supposed to go. What would you like?"

"It would be great if you could check your phone," Jazz said, looking at the crowd. Karin nodded in agreement.

Rosie flipped through her phone. "Grade eight, last name Sidhu. Your homeroom is room 213 with

Mr. Leitch." She pointed at a staircase that led to the second floor. "Up those stairs, second room on the right."

"What about me?" Karin asked. "My last name is Santos."

Rosie quickly checked the list. "Good news! You're in the same homeroom as Jazz. Do you want one of us to walk you there, or will you be okay?"

"Thanks," said Jazz. "We will be fine."

The two friends walked up the stairs. When they arrived at room 213 it was full of new Grade Eight students. Jazz didn't know any of them.

"Welcome to Northside." A teacher walked into the room carrying a plastic tote full of papers. "I'm Mr. Leitch. I teach Math at Northside, including a block of grade eight Math. Maybe I'll see some of you in my class."

He put the tote down onto his desk. "Everyone have a phone or a tablet?" he asked.

All the students did. "Okay, then. Here's how you download the app. It has all the school information you need, including notifications, the Code of Conduct and the bell schedule. You can also use the calendar feature to remind yourself of homework due dates and tests."

The class downloaded the app quickly. Once they were done, Mr. Leitch started calling out names. "First up is Karin Santos. Where are you, Karin?"

Karin quickly put her hand up.

"Excellent," said Mr. Leitch, as he handed her a piece of paper. "Here's your timetable. If you want to know where your classrooms are, just ask me or one of the LINK crew when they take you on your tour. The building looks big, but you'll find your way around it well enough after a couple of days.

Mr. Leitch looked at the next timetable. "Joey Sargent? Where are you?"

Within five minutes all the students had their timetables, including Jazz.

"That's about it from me," said Mr. Leitch. "In five minutes, you're going to be called down to the gym to hear words of wisdom from Ms. Webb, the principal. Then you'll be off for a quick tour. After that you get to go home and enjoy the sunshine. And don't get stressed," he added. "You may be a little overwhelmed right now. But within a week it will feel like you were always a Raven."

Karin and Jazz quickly compared timetables. For her first semester, Jazz had English, Home Economics, Math and French. Her second semester classes were Science, Social Studies, PE and Technology Education.

"Can you believe it?" Karin said disappointedly. "Eight classes and not one together. At least you have Mr. Leitch for Math. He seems like a nice guy."

Jazz realized some of what she was feeling must be showing on her face. Karin asked, "Are you okay?"

"I'm fine," said Jazz. But she was not. She knew PE

would be on her timetable, but seeing it there made her feel a little queasy. Most of her troubles in elementary school had been in that class. But back then she had Karin to look out for her.

"Do you want me to see Ms. Yao and ask if we can be put in the same PE class?"

For the millionth time Jazz felt glad Karin was her friend. It was as if Karin could read her mind. And while a part of her wanted to be in the same class as Karin, she didn't want to cause work for anyone.

"No," said Jazz. "Second semester doesn't start for five months. I'm sure things will be fine by then."

"Whatever you want," Karin said. "Just don't forget, I have your back."

A voice came over the school intercom. "At this time, could all grade eights please make their way to the gym." With Mr. Leitch leading the class, they headed to the gym. Soon all the grade eights, more than three hundred of them, were sitting in the bleachers.

Jazz felt better in the Northside gym when she took a seat in the familiar bleachers. As Ms. Webb welcomed them to the school, Jazz paid more attention to the blue-and-gold championship banners hanging on the wall than what the principal was saying. Akisha had helped win the latest one, and had even been tournament MVP. Jazz was proud of her sister. But she couldn't help feel like she didn't live up to her sister when compared to her.

The First Day

After Ms. Webb's speech, the LINK Leaders took each homeroom around the school. Jazz was happy to see that Franca was the one assigned to show her class around. Jazz had spent plenty of time in the gym, but had never seen the computer labs, the art classes and most of the other rooms. She made notes of where her classrooms were. She hoped she would remember where to go when school started for real the next day.

"That's it, everyone," said Franca when she led the grade eights back to the gym. "Don't forget that we are available to help tomorrow and the rest of the week. Go home and have fun."

"I don't know about you, Karin, but I hope I don't get . . ." Before Jazz could finish the sentence, her heart stopped. Not three metres away, standing in the middle of a group of girls, was the last person Jazz thought she would see again. She'd grown taller and had changed her hair, but it was Mia Hanson. Their eyes locked. Mia gave Jazz a cold look, then turned away.

"Hope you don't what?" Then Karin saw as well. "Mia? What's she doing here? Her parents sent her to private school after the problems she caused you!"

Jazz felt like throwing up. "I guess she came back."

3 Nothing Wrong WITH JAZZ

That night, Jazz's mom grilled steaks. Steak was one of Jazz's favourite foods of all time, but she was hardly able to eat a thing. "Are you okay?" her mom asked.

Jazz pushed some peas around the plate with her fork. "I'm fine, just tired from the first day of school. Maybe I have a stomach bug or something."

"You can't be sick of school already," her mom joked. "You were only there for two hours today!"

"I'm sure I'll be fine." Jazz didn't believe a word of what she said. She wasn't sick of school. She didn't have a stomach bug. And she certainly wasn't going to be fine. It was Mia, back in her life, that had upset her. She almost told her mom. But she decided against it. What could she do about it? The stuff with Mia from before had upset her mom as much as it had Jazz. Better to not worry her.

Jazz excused herself from the table. "I think I'm going to go to bed." Without waiting for a response, Jazz left the dining room and ran up the stairs to her room.

She shut the door and flung herself on the bed. Then she messaged Karin. The two girls talked for hours. Karin came up with ideas of how they could deal with the situation. Some were good. Others, like moving to Florida or asking aliens to kidnap Mia, were less realistic. By nine o'clock, Jazz was exhausted. She'd been worrying about Mia for more than eight hours. Despite thinking she would be up all night, Jazz fell asleep five minutes after turning off her phone.

★★★

As things turned out, it wasn't as bad as Jazz feared — at least not at first. Her elementary school had been small. Back then, Mia had been in her class and Jazz had to see her every day, all day. Northside was different. Jazz didn't have any classes with Mia. Though she would see Mia sometimes, it was from a distance, or when they were both in the Commons, and it was easy enough to avoid her there. Jazz was also relieved that, with the exception of a few mean looks, there was no contact between them at all.

Mr. Leitch was right as well. Within a week, Jazz knew her way around the school. She knew her teachers and had even made a couple of new friends. By the time September was over and the leaves on the maple and cherry trees on her street started to turn orange and yellow, Jazz felt like she'd always been at Northside.

Things were going great, in fact. But then Jazz's mom dropped a bomb on her when they were eating dinner.

"How was school today, dear?" her mom asked as she dished up. "What interesting things did you do?"

"Nothing much." That was Jazz's standard response. School had been going fine but she didn't want to share every detail with her parent.

"I was looking at the school website today," her mom said a few minutes later. She spoke between mouthfuls of spaghetti and meatballs. "I saw something interesting."

Something interesting, Jazz thought. "Like what?" Jazz knew how her mom worked. She was instantly on her guard.

"All sorts of things, actually. Parent-teacher night is next week. The drama teacher is auditioning for the musical. And there are some interesting clubs at your school."

"That's it?" asked Jazz suspiciously. Her mom was up to something and she knew it.

"Well, there was something else," her mom added. "I couldn't help but read that basketball season is coming up. I was thinking that maybe you would change your mind and try out. What do you think?"

"Are you kidding me?" Jazz felt like screaming. "How many times do we have to have this talk?"

"I called Karin's mom earlier," her mom said. "You two have been shooting hoops together since you were in diapers. You're as good as Karin, maybe even better. I don't see why you won't at least give it a try."

"You know how I feel about this." Jazz was trying her very best not to get upset. It wasn't easy.

"I talked to your sister about it, too," said her mom. "Akisha agrees. She wants you to play. She knows you can do it."

"You talked to Akisha about me playing basketball? Why are you all ganging up on me?" Jazz could feel her cheeks burning with anger.

"Nobody is ganging up on you," said her mom, trying to smooth things over. "But you are letting your past stand in the way of you becoming your best future self. You know how far you've come. You need to put it in the rear-view mirror."

Jazz couldn't believe what she was hearing. "My best future self? The rear-view mirror? Focus on the future? You've been reading too many self-help books."

"Maybe you should read them, Jaspreet," her mom snapped in Punjabi. Jazz knew her mom was getting angry when she called her by her full name. And they mostly used English at home, but when her mom got worked up, she spoke in her first language. But her mom caught herself and said in a calmer voice, "There is nothing wrong with you, Jazz. Everybody has something to overcome. You have had so many advantages. Many people have had a tougher life than you, have had to overcome harder things. You have been lucky growing up in Canada. You take things for granted. You don't know what it was like back in India when I was a child."

Back in India. Jazz cringed. That was one of the other sayings she hated. Whenever Jazz complained about something, her mom would reply with "back in India we . . ." Jazz had done her best to contain herself but the comment was the last straw.

"I don't care what it was like for you growing up in India, Mom!"

She pushed back her chair and stormed out of the dining room, a half-eaten meatball on her plate. "When will you get it? I'm never playing basketball! Not for Northside. Not any team. Never!"

4 Karin's PROBLEM

"What's wrong, Karin?" Jazz knew something was up with her friend the second she saw her in the Commons the next Monday. Jazz had been friends with Karin since before kindergarten and knew her better than anyone.

"Nothing," Karin said. They sat down at their usual table to eat lunch. "At least nothing you need to worry about."

"Karin! How can you even say that? When have we ever not worried about each other?"

"Are you sure, Jazz? I don't think you want to hear it."

"There is nothing you could say that I wouldn't want to hear," said Jazz. "You're my best friend."

Karin took a deep breath. "Okay. It's the basketball team."

Jazz knew Karin had signed up to play, just as Karin knew Jazz hadn't. Karin hadn't put any pressure on Jazz to join.

"You didn't get cut, did you?" Jazz knew Karin was a strong player. If she got cut, it would surprise her.

"No, nothing like that," Karin said. "Kind of the opposite, really. Our first practice was last Friday. We had eleven girls come out. But we lost our two best players today."

"What happened?"

"Stephanie's moving. Her dad got transferred to Kelowna. They leave next week. When Stephanie told us she was leaving Northside, Taylor quit as well. She said that, without Stephanie, we wouldn't do very well. So Taylor's just going to play for her club team."

No wonder Karin is upset, thought Jazz. Stephanie and Taylor were the best basketball players in grade eight. The team would be a lot weaker without them.

"We're carrying on," said Karin. "But we could have won the district championship. Now I'll be surprised if we have a winning record at all this year."

There was no more talk of basketball that lunchtime. When the bell rang, Jazz and Karin said goodbye to each other and went off to their classes.

Jazz went to Math class. She was happy Mr. Leitch was her teacher. Jazz had always struggled at math. Sometimes the numbers and the letters didn't make any sense to her at all. But Mr. Leitch had a way of explaining things so she could understand them. It was also great that he was funny.

Karin's Problem

The next morning, Jazz and Karin walked to school together. It was a typical Vancouver fall day. The rain fell from a grey, cloudy sky. The wind blew hard on the few brown leaves that still clung to the trees. Jazz could see that Karin's mood matched the weather.

"I don't believe it, Jazz," she said. "We're having the worst luck ever!"

The Grade Eight girls' basketball team had lost another member. Kiara, a guard on the team, had twisted her ankle badly in practice. She would be out for at least two months.

"How many players do you have left?" asked Jazz.

"Eight. Not that it matters. Kiara was the best three-point shooter on the team."

"No, she wasn't," said Jazz. She tried to find something to cheer her friend up. "You're way better. Don't worry. Your team will be fine."

But by the end of Wednesday, things were definitely not fine for the Grade Eight girls Northside Ravens.

Karin was near tears when the two girls met in Mr. Leitch's homeroom to pick up their first report card of the year. "I'm going to quit before something bad happens to me, Jazz. The team is cursed."

The basketball team was down to six players. Two girls, Grace and Christine, had got into a nasty fight over social media. Both had posted cruel things about each other and screenshots of their posts had been sent to Ms. Webb and Ms. Fridge, the team coach. The school's code of conduct was clear. Such online behaviour had serious consequences. For Grace and Christine, those consequences included being removed from the team.

"Here you go, Jazz," said Mr. Leitch as he handed out report cards. "Not bad. Not bad at all! Looks like you made the honour roll,"

Jazz was sad for Karin about the basketball team. But she was very happy for herself when she saw her report card. Three As in her other classes and a B in Math. Jazz had never had such good grades. How could she ever have been nervous about high school?

By Thursday morning the basketball team was down to five girls. Jazz had never seen Karin so upset. Zoey, another guard, had brought home a bad report card and her parents had pulled her from the team to focus on her schoolwork.

"We can't run a team with only five players," said Karin. "We won't have any subs. And if someone is hurt or can't make a game, we would either have to forfeit or play short-handed. Coach Fridge has called a team meeting at lunch. It looks like the season is over before it even began. If we don't get more players, the girls' team is finished."

5 Jazz's DECISION

No matter how hard she tried, Jazz couldn't get the talk with Karin out of her head. *If we don't get more players, the girls' team is finished.* Jazz looked at her phone. It was almost two in the morning. She had been tossing and turning, thinking about what her friend had said.

Karin was heartbroken about the basketball situation. But the good friend she was, she never once pressured Jazz to join. Karin understood what Jazz had gone through with her disorder. Karin had been a true friend to Jazz for years. Jazz owed her more than she could ever hope to repay. Jazz always said she would do anything for Karin. It was then the little voice in her head, the little voice her mom always talked about, whispered to her. Jazz hated it, hated it more than anything. But Jazz knew the little voice was right. There was something she could do after all.

Right after English in A Block, Jazz went to the gym before heading to Mr. Estabrook's Home Economics class.

"Ms. Fridge, can I talk to you?" she asked.

Ms. Fridge, a friendly looking teacher in a Northside Ravens track suit, greeted Jazz warmly. "Of course," said Ms. Fridge. "You look familiar. But I don't think I know you, do I?"

"My name's Jazz Sidhu. I'm in grade eight."

"Sidhu. You must be Akisha's sister. She was in my Leadership class last year. I love Akisha! How's she doing?"

Of course, thought Jazz. Everyone loved her sister at Northside. "Akisha's fine. But I was wondering if I could talk to you about basketball. Karin says that the team might fold."

Ms. Fridge nodded. "We've had some bad luck, that's for sure. We have just five girls left. I don't think we can run a program with that few. I asked the girls to reach out to their friends to see if anybody else wants to join. But no one has come forward yet."

Karin hadn't asked Jazz to play, even with the team about to be cancelled. What an amazing friend, Jazz thought.

"You've got time, though," Jazz said. "Karin told me the first game isn't for three weeks. You should be able to find more players by then."

I sure hope you can, she thought. She tried to ignore the little voice in her head. It was whispering the night before, but was speaking louder now.

"That's true," said Ms. Fridge. "But I have to send

the team roster to BC School Sports by three p.m. today. Anyone who joins after that can't play league games or playoffs. Were you thinking of coming out, Jazz?" asked Ms. Fridge hopefully. "We sure could use you."

Jazz cringed. The little voice in her head was yelling at her very loudly. "I'm not very good."

"Don't worry about that. I teach the basic skills. And if you're anything like your sister, I'm sure you are better than you think."

The little voice inside Jazz's head was now shouting. "I wouldn't want to let the team down."

"Don't be concerned about that either," Ms. Fridge reassured Jazz. "I'm a competitive coach and I like to win. But at grade eight level, I'm much more focused on team building, learning basic skills and developing a good work ethic. We may not win every game and you may not be the best player on the team. But you will build your character and your skills, and become a better person for it."

Jazz took a deep breath. I'll do this for Karin, she thought, even if it kills me.

"Okay," she said. She could hardly believe the words when she spoke them. "I'll try."

Ms. Fridge beamed. "Awesome! Six players isn't much, but it's a heck of a lot better than five. I'll put your name on the roster. We practise after school today. It looks like we may have a season after all."

The only person happier than Ms. Fridge was Karin when Jazz told her the news at lunch.

"Thank you so much!" Karin cried and hugged Jazz so tightly Jazz could hardly breathe. "How did you know to see Coach Fridge? She asked us to talk to our friends but I . . ."

". . . never asked me." Jazz finished the sentence for her.

"I wouldn't have either," Karin said. "Your friendship is worth more to me than basketball. Besides, I know how you feel about being pressured by your mom to play."

"Your friendship is worth more than that, too," said Jazz. "Ms. Fridge said that, with six players, the team can play."

"We might even have seven," Karin said. "Elisha messaged me ten minutes ago and said she thinks she has another girl interested."

"Who?" Jazz asked.

"She didn't tell me her name," said Karin. "But she's supposed to be good. Who knows? Not only are we going to have a team, we may actually even win a couple of games this season!"

6 SURPRISE!

Jazz had never felt so nervous as when she arrived at the gym for her first practice. She took a deep breath, then stepped through the doors onto the hardwood floor. Not as a spectator, not as a student, but as a member of the Northside Ravens basketball team.

She'd also never felt more welcome.

"Jazz!" cried Karin, as she ran to Jazz and hugged her tightly. Soon Jazz was surrounded by the other girls. They patted her on the back and hugged her, with big smiles all around.

"Hi, Elisha! Hi, Cerys!" Jazz said. "Hi, everybody."

Elisha and Cerys had gone to elementary school with Jazz as well. But she didn't know the other two girls.

"I'm Kianna," said a small, black-haired girl.

"Hannah," said the other, a tall girl with long blonde hair in a ponytail.

"Welcome, Jazz!" Ms. Fridge walked into the gym. She had a clipboard in her hand and a whistle around her neck. "I just emailed the roster to BC School Sports. You are officially on our team of seven." She started counting. "I see six of you, but where is our other new . . ."

"Sorry I'm late."

Jazz heard the voice behind her and froze. She knew that voice. She had heard it for years, both in real life and her nightmares. Of all the students in this school, it had to be her.

"Welcome, Mia," said Ms. Fridge. "Everyone, this is Mia Hanson."

Kianna and Hannah greeted Mia with the same friendly manner they'd shown Jazz. Elisha and Cerys knew the history between Mia and Jazz. They stood there, looking uncomfortable. Karin ran to Jazz and stood protectively beside her.

Ms. Fridge seemed oblivious to the drama and carried on. "Thanks again for coming out, Jazz and Mia. We wouldn't have had a season without you. Now gather round and let's get warmed up properly. I can't afford to have any of you hurt!"

With Ms. Fridge leading them, the girls got into a circle and stretched. Karin stayed right beside Jazz. Karin's eyes were locked on Mia, who was stretching almost directly across from them.

When they were done stretching, Ms. Fridge rolled out a cart of basketballs. "Partner up and pass to each other," she said.

Surprise!

The girls quickly paired up. Mia was left without a partner.

"Mia, you can join Karin and Jazz," Ms. Fridge said. "With an uneven number, we'll make one group of three."

Jazz couldn't believe that Mia had been paired with her and Karin. She felt funny inside. It was almost like the time she'd eaten too much candy and popcorn at the movies and got sick.

"Don't worry. You got this," Karin said. She passed the ball to Jazz with a perfectly aimed bounce pass.

Despite the trembling in her hands, Jazz caught the ball and quickly tossed it to Mia. The throw wasn't her best by any means, and Mia had to slide to the side to catch it. Mia quickly threw the ball back to Jazz. The pass wasn't hard, but Jazz fumbled it as it neared her chest. The ball dropped, hit her knee and rolled off the court.

Jazz picked up the ball. Mia didn't laugh at her for dropping the ball. But Jazz heard the echoes of a thousand other times Mia had made fun of her.

Five minutes later, Ms. Fridge blew her whistle. "That's good enough for now, girls. Huddle up and let's continue working on the play we started last practice."

With the team gathered around her she began. "The play is called Thunderbird. I learned it when I played for the University of British Columbia. It's a simple screen and roll. But we should be able to score a lot of points if we do it well. Let's review the floor positions and run through the play a few times. Karin is the point guard. Elisha is the shooting guard. Kianna and Cerys play forwards. Hannah plays centre. Got it? We'll rotate positions through the season, but let's try this first."

Ms. Fridge turned to Mia and Jazz. "Stand on the sidelines and watch for now. I'll sub you both in soon."

Jazz took a spot three metres away from Mia. She tried to ignore her but it still felt like Mia was hovering right over her back.

"Let's run it," said Ms. Fridge. Jazz listened carefully as the coach set up the play. This part of the game had always been the hardest for her. "Cerys and Hannah, set up positions two metres away from each other at the top of the key. Hannah on the left and Cerys on the right."

The girls did as they were told. Ms. Fridge brought in Elisha and Kianna. "Elisha," said Ms. Fridge, "set yourself up halfway between the sideline and Hannah. Kianna, you do the same thing but on Cerys's side."

Ms. Fridge watched with approval as the girls got into position. "Excellent," she said. "Karin, you take the ball, stand at the centre line and get ready to run the play. Trust me, it's easy."

Jazz felt her panic grow. This was shaping up to be very hard, no matter what the coach said. Shooting hoops in the driveway was easy. Thunderbird, or whatever stupid name the coach gave the play, was not.

"You can run Thunderbird on either side of the court," Ms. Fridge told the team. "First time through, Karin is going to run it to Cerys's side. When she does, Hannah rolls towards Karin to set up a screen. Then, Cerys is going to stand in the key near the net. The expression in basketball is posting up. You got that?"

The girls nodded, even Jazz, who definitely didn't get it.

"Great," said Ms. Fridge. "Karin now has the choice of going in for a layup or taking a shot behind the screen. If neither of those options work, she can feed it to Cerys under the basket or pass it to the outside to Kianna or Elisha. We'll practise each one, starting with the layup. Take your time. Focus on positioning and accurate passing."

The team ran the play for several minutes, with Karin either shooting the ball herself or passing it to each of the other girls. Then the moment Jazz had been dreading came. "Jazz, take Hannah's spot. Mia, you take Cerys's."

Jazz trotted onto the court. She passed by Karin, who was standing at centre court, ball in her hand. "You got this, Jazz," Karin said.

Karin drove to the right. Jazz's brain knew she had to roll over to set a screen for Karin. But sending the message from her brain to her feet was another matter. Jazz froze for a second. Then, instead of screening Karin, Jazz ran to the high post. She nearly knocked Mia over as she did.

"You're supposed to set the screen," said Mia. They were the first words she had spoken to Jazz all year. "Like Coach said, it's not hard. For most people."

"Don't worry about it, Jazz," encouraged Ms. Fridge. "We'll run it again."

Jazz hurried back to her position. This time she got it right, rolling over to set a screen as Karin passed the ball to Kianna for a nice jumpshot. But it took every little bit of concentration she had.

When practice ended an hour later, Jazz was more tired than she'd been in years. Not physically tired. Jazz was used to working hard. But she was mentally tired from having to concentrate on the play. It felt as if her brain was about to explode. Jazz was upset as well. Not only was Mia on the team but Jazz had made a fool of herself in front of her. The little voice inside her head had told Jazz to play. But that stupid little voice wasn't giving her any help right now.

7 Promise
MADE

"It's not your fault, Karin," said Jazz. From the moment Jazz and her best friend left the gym to walk home, Karin had been telling Jazz how sorry she was. "You didn't ask me to join. And you didn't know Mia was the other girl."

"I shouldn't have even told you the team was in trouble." Jazz had never seen Karin so upset. "She's so awful. I can't believe I put you in this position."

"It's okay. Really, it is," said Jazz, but it wasn't.

When Mia had stepped into the gym, it was all Jazz could do to not turn and run. Then things went from bad to worse when Jazz messed up the play. It's not hard. For most people. The words stung. Jazz was trapped. All she wanted to do was quit. But if she did, the team could fold and Karin would miss out. Plus, Jazz had promised the coach she would play.

If Jazz quit, she would disappoint her friend and her new coach. If she stuck with it, she was doomed to play with the person who had made her life miserable for years.

"I'll message you later, Karin," said Jazz when they reached Ellerslie Avenue.

The friends said goodbye and Jazz walked up the path to her house. The first thing she saw when she opened the front door was her mom with a huge grin on her face.

"You joined the team!" Her mom looked as if she would burst with happiness. "Karin's mom called me. I'm so proud of you! If you hadn't stepped up, they wouldn't have a team."

Jazz sat on the couch and fought back the tears. She had not told her mother about signing up for basketball. She hadn't planned on telling her until she figured out what she was going to do. Things kept getting worse.

"So did Mia."

"Mia?" Her mom looked confused. "That Mia? What on earth is she doing at Northside? I thought she moved." Her mom switched to Punjabi. She did that when she was upset as well as angry. "When? Why didn't you tell me, Jaspreet?"

"She started in September with the rest of us. I didn't tell you because I didn't want you to worry. I'm older now, and I wanted to deal with it myself."

"I'll make tea," said her mom.

Jazz suddenly felt a tiny bit better. She'd wanted to tell her mom Mia was at Northside a hundred times, but had never done it. The bullying had been as hard on her mom as it had been for Jazz. Her mom liked being in control of things. Protecting her family was very important to her. Jazz knew her mom had felt terrible about it. Like she'd let down Jazz because she hadn't been able to stop the bullying.

Jazz's mom came back with the tea. It was spicy, hot and steaming, full of milk and sugar, just the way Jazz liked it.

"Be honest, Jaspreet," said her mom. "Have there been any problems with Mia since she came back?"

"No, not really," Jazz said. It's not hard. For most people. The comment was hurtful. But it was nothing compared to what Mia had done and said in the past.

"So maybe she's changed," her mom suggested hopefully.

"I doubt that very much," said Jazz.

"What are you going to do? I would understand if you wanted to quit the team."

"And let Karin and the others down? Besides, I made a promise." Jazz was so frustrated by wrestling with the whole thing. She wished someone else could deal with it. "I want to quit. But I told the coach I would play. I can't back out now without letting people down. Can't you just tell me what to do?"

Her mom took a sip of tea and then shook her head. "I will support you no matter what you do, Jazz, but this decision has to be yours."

★★★

After dinner, Jazz excused herself, picked up her basketball and went outside. It was dark, and a light October drizzle hung in the air. But Jazz needed to shoot hoops. She was out there by herself for half an hour, taking shot after shot. She was still trying to figure out what to do when her phone rang.

Jazz took the phone from her pocket and looked at the number. Her heart leaped. Akisha! She messaged her sister every day. But she hadn't talked to her for almost a week. "Hey, big sister," she said. "How are you?"

"Mom told me you decided to play ball for Northside," Akisha said. Her voice came clearly through the phone like she was next door instead of four thousand kilometres away. "I thought you were never going to play. What made you change your mind?"

"The little voice inside my head." It was raining harder now. The drizzle had turned to bigger drops. It was cold as well. Jazz was getting soaked and she could see her breath in the light from the street lamp. But she was so happy to talk to Akisha that she didn't care.

"Mom also told me about Mia. What are you going to do?"

"I don't know." Jazz really didn't. One minute she was certain that quitting was her only option. Two minutes later she had changed her mind and was determined to stick it out. "What do you think?" Akisha would know. She would tell her what to do.

"I can't make that choice for you," she said.

Jazz groaned. Her mom had said the exact same thing.

"Here's what I think, though," Akisha added. "When I played ball in high school, there were girls on the team I would never have hung out with, let alone become friends with. But the funny thing is that sometimes the love of a sport can bring very different people together."

Not for one minute did Jazz believe that would happen.

"Tell me," Akisha said. "Mia — is she good at basketball?"

"She's okay." Jazz had to admit that Mia was pretty good from what she'd seen.

"Then you never know," said Akisha. "You'll do the right thing, I know it. I'm proud of you, little sister."

Jazz felt warmth go through her at the compliment, despite the rain.

"I have to go now," Akisha said. "It's three hours later here than in Vancouver, and I have a mid-term exam tomorrow. Message me and let me know how it goes."

Jazz hung up and went inside to dry off. She felt better knowing her family would support whatever she decided to do. She just wished she knew what that was. Jazz had another cup of tea with her mom then went to bed. It wasn't until much later that she finally made a decision — one she knew she would regret.

8 Last Pick
AGAIN

"Can I have number seven?" asked Jazz. Ms. Fridge was passing out the jerseys. Akisha always wore number seven, after Kevin Durant, her favourite player.

"Your sister's number," said the coach. She gave Jazz a white home jersey and a black away one. Both had large sevens on their backs. "I figured you'd want to wear that one."

"Number seven for player number seven." Mia said it under her breath, just loud enough for Jazz to hear. Jazz's cheeks burned. Mia didn't say seventh best out of seven. She could have meant the seventh player to sign up. But Jazz knew exactly what Mia meant. Last choice. Last Pick. Again. Jazz fought the urge to toss the jerseys on the floor and leave the gym, but she had given her word. Instead, she put them in her backpack and took her place at centre court. Ms. Fridge was standing there, waiting to teach the girls another play.

"You've done a great job with Thunderbird," said Ms. Fridge. "Today we are going to learn two more plays.

The three plays will be the basis of our offence this season. The first is a play I call Raven. It's a Ms. Yao original. Raven sets us up for a layup if the other team is playing person-to-person defence. The other play is a three-point-shot play called Viking. The University of Victoria women's team are masters of this one. Since they've won nine national championships, I think it's worth learning."

Jazz felt a lump grow in her throat. Learning one play last practice nearly killed her. How on earth did Coach Fridge think she was capable of learning two? In one day?

They began with Raven. Ms. Fridge told the girls where to stand, then waited as they got into position. Jazz stood in front of Mia, her back to the net, hoping that she wouldn't have to do anything except watch.

Once they were in position, Ms. Fridge told them what each girl was to do. "Like Thunderbird, you can run this play to the right or the left of the court in a game. But for now, let's start with the right side and change up once you have the basics. Sound good, Karin?"

"Sounds good, Coach." Karin stood in her position, ready to go. Jazz admired her friend's confidence.

"Jazz and Karin, make your moves," said Ms. Fridge. Jazz focused as hard as she could, trying to remember what to do. Baseline! I run to the baseline and help Mia set up a screen! Jazz moved, focusing so hard on following directions her head hurt. Don't screw this up in front of Mia, she thought as both girls moved down to the baseline.

"Now it's your turn, Kianna," said Ms. Fridge. Kianna ran down the court and took up her position behind her screen. "The play is a double-fake. We've started by convincing the defence that the ball will go to Kianna. Now we are going to confuse them by having Elisha hustle out to the top of the key."

With a big smile on her face, Elisha did just that.

Ms. Fridge continued. "Karin, you dribble in, fake a pass to Elisha, then fake another pass to Kianna. Their defence will scramble. Elisha then cuts back into the key, where you give her the ball and she goes in for the easy layup. Sound good?"

It sounded terribly confusing to Jazz. She was grateful all she had to do was set up the screen.

"Okay, then," said Ms. Fridge. "Get back to your starting positions. Walk through it a couple of times and then run the play at game speed."

Set the screen, Jazz told herself. That's all I have to do for now. I can do this. She ignored Mia, who was right beside her with a nasty grin on her face. Jazz ran to the baseline, her hands up, as Kianna cut behind her. Jazz concentrated as hard as she ever had in her life.

She heard Ms. Fridge blow the whistle. She heard the squeak of shoe on hardwood as the girls ran. She heard Karin bounce the ball as she started the play. She heard Elisha call for the ball. She watched as Elisha cut back to the hoop where she took the pass and went in for the easy bucket.

"Great job!" exclaimed Ms. Fridge. "See, I told you it was easy. Let's do it a few more times. Then we will change up positions."

It was easy, Jazz thought as they ran the play. Easy because all she had to do was run to the baseline and stand there. But then Ms. Fridge blew the whistle and changed things up.

"Jazz, you take Kianna's spot and Mia take Elisha's. Kianna and Elisha sub off and let Cerys and Hannah set up the screen."

Jazz had hoped she would be subbed off. Instead she had to move to a different position. She took a deep breath as a drop of sweat rolled down her face. Plan your movement. Think it through, talk it through. Those were strategies Jazz had learned in therapy. This time I have to run behind the screen and set up for a pass. Easy. You can do this, she told herself. The whistle blew. Karin dribbled left.

"Now, Jazz," said Ms. Fridge.

Jazz turned and began to sprint as Hannah and Cerys set up the screen. Then it happened. Somehow her left foot got tangled up in her right foot. She stumbled, falling awkwardly to the court floor.

"Are you okay, Jazz?" asked Ms. Fridge.

Jazz hurried to her feet, her cheeks burning with embarrassment. "I'm fine."

"Happens all the time," said Ms. Fridge. She got a towel and wiped Jazz's sweat off the hardwood. "If I had a dollar for every time I fell on the floor, I'd be a millionaire."

"You'd be a billionaire, Jazz," Mia whispered.

"What did you say, Mia?" Karin had hurried over to help Jazz to her feet. Mia had made her comment under her breath but both Jazz and Karin had heard it well enough.

"Just joking," Mia said. "Coach is right. It could happen to anyone."

"Let's run it again," said Coach Fridge. If the coach was aware of the drama starting to build, she didn't draw attention to it.

"I'm ready," Jazz said, getting back into position.

Slowly, and with her eyes locked on Mia, Karin returned to centre court. This time Jazz didn't fall. She ran the play perfectly, watching as Karin faked and then dished the ball into Mia, who went up for the layup. Mia banked the ball perfectly off the glass and it fell in for the basket.

"Well done, everyone," said Ms. Fridge. "We'll run it a few more times and then move on to Viking!"

An hour later, the practice ended. Jazz felt as if her head were about to explode. Fakes, cuts, dishes, down screens, elevator screens. It was almost too much for her to take.

"You did really well, Jazz," said Karin as the two girls walked home. It was getting dark and had started to rain. "Don't let Mia get to you. You're a better player than she is. She's just jealous of you."

"Thanks." Jazz didn't believe it. Mia made layups. Mia got the plays first time around. Mia didn't trip over her own two feet.

"Walk to school tomorrow?" Karin asked as they reached Jazz's driveway.

"Sure," said Jazz. "Tomorrow."

As Karin carried on down the street, Jazz opened the garage door and put down her backpack. There was nothing in it but a math book and her jerseys, but Jazz had felt the weight of it since leaving school. Akisha wore number seven. Akisha had been a star at school. But here was Jazz, wearing the same number and stumbling on the court like she was a toddler learning to walk. She picked up her basketball. The rain came down harder as she walked through the plays she'd learned at practice, taking her turns in each position.

"What on earth are you doing, Jazz?" Her mom must have heard the garage door open. She was standing in the front door. "It's pouring outside. Come in and have dinner."

"Ten minutes," said Jazz, as she went in for a layup. The ball slipped from her fingers and hit the outside of the rim. "I need to practise a bit more."

Jazz was hungry and exhausted. She wanted to quit, to go to her room and cry. But she had made a promise and she knew she had to stick with it.

No matter what.

9 Defence IS HARD

It had been hard, but Jazz learned the three offence plays. Ms. Fridge taught them another play as well, but Jazz had no problems with this one. The play was called Raptor and it was all about Karin. Karin would call that play if she saw a hole in the defence. Then she would drive to the hoop by herself and go for the shot. Jazz hoped that Karin would use Raptor a lot.

At the last practice before the first game of the season, Jazz found that defence was something else. It took everything she had not to run off the floor in tears.

Some junior girls had come to practice to help Ms. Fridge. "Hard to practise defending if there isn't a team to defend against," she said. The juniors were nice enough, but they were bigger and faster than the grade eights. Jazz felt intimidated playing against them. But what was worse was learning the plays at all.

Person-to-person defence was simple enough. You chose a player from the other team and stuck to them, trying your best to keep them from passing or shooting.

But zone defence? Jazz's head was spinning — 3-2 set, 1-2-1, triangle defence, chameleon defence, junk defence. Then there was the half-court press and the full-court press.

It was terrible. Jazz felt like she was trying to learn a foreign language.

"It's okay, Jazz," Ms. Fridge said for what seemed like the hundredth time. "Next time stand near the baseline, not the top of the key."

Jazz felt lost. She didn't know whether to slide right or left, what position to take on the court, what person to pick up. The worst part was Mia. Jazz could see her roll her eyes and shake her head when Jazz made a mistake. She could hear her mutter things under her breath. By the end of the practice Jazz was exhausted.

"Don't worry about it," said Karin as they walked home together. "I was getting confused, too. We all were. Defence is hard."

Jazz was quiet at dinner. Then she excused herself from the table and went to her room. Ms. Fridge had given the girls sheets of paper with the defences drawn up on them. Jazz knew she should review them, but didn't have the energy. Instead she picked up her phone and called her sister.

Seven p.m. in Vancouver was ten at night in Toronto. Akisha would still be awake. Jazz needed to talk, to hear her sister's voice, to be reassured. But Akisha didn't answer. And she didn't return Jazz's text.

Too busy with her new, perfect life. Too busy to help Jazz. Jazz lay in bed, waiting for the little voice to tell her what to do. But it didn't say a word.

Friday came. The first game of the season was an exhibition match against Eagle Mountain at home. As Jazz stepped onto the court, she felt like throwing up. She wore her sister's number seven on her back. Jazz had thought the number would be comforting to her. Instead, the number felt like it weighed a ton. Jazz looked up to the bleachers and saw her mom. Then she looked at the banners above the hardwood floor. Akisha had worn that same number and led the team to a provincial championship. Her sister was an all-star. But Jazz didn't know whether to turn right or left on the court. She felt like a fraud.

"Jazz? Is everything all right?" Ms. Fridge was looking at Jazz, concern all over her face.

"I don't feel very well," said Jazz. "I'm not sure I can play."

"We'll keep you on the bench for the start of the game and see how you feel in a bit. How does that sound?" asked her coach.

It sounded terrible to Jazz. But at least she wouldn't have to start the game and embarrass herself right away. "Fine," she said, not meaning it at all.

The teams warmed up, taking shots, running drills as the clock ran down. With one minute left until game time, the horn sounded. The girls on both teams hustled back to their benches.

"Do your best and work hard," said Ms. Fridge. "Exhibition games are where we work out the bugs. But that doesn't mean we take them lightly. Jazz and Elisha, you start on the bench while the rest of you take your places on the court. Now let's give a cheer and get out there and play!"

The horn sounded. The ref blew her whistle and tossed the ball high into the air between Hannah and the Eagle Mountain centre. Hannah was first to the ball. She tipped it back to Mia, who quickly passed to Karin.

Jazz could sense the excitement and the energy all around her. The crowd wasn't large. It was mostly the parents of the players, including her own mom, dressed in her Ravens hoodie. Eagle Mountain parents were there as well, dressed in their team's black and gold.

Ms. Fridge stood in front of the bench, directing the play. "Raven!" she shouted.

Karin dribbled across the centre line. She nodded and waited for the rest of the team to take their positions, and then made her move. She dribbled to the right and waited for the girls to cut and run and overload the left side. The fake worked to perfection. Mia, who was in the three position, cut back, took the pass and went in for the easy layup. Her basket made the score Ravens 2, Eagle Mountain Talons 0.

Jazz cheered from the bench. Maybe joining the team wasn't a bad idea after all.

10 Jazz SUBS IN

Eagle Mountain scored on their first possession. They made a nice jumpshot from just inside the three-point line to tie the game at two points.

Jazz watched from the bench as the game went back and forth. The teams were evenly matched. Despite her nerves, Jazz felt slightly better to see many of the girls making some mistakes. Two minutes into the game, Karin lost the ball when an Eagle Mountain player poked it from her hands and ran down the court for a layup. Jazz felt bad for thinking it, but she was almost happy to see Mia miss a wide open shot just under the basket on the next offensive set for the Ravens.

By the end of the first quarter, the teams were tied 12–12.

"Good job, girls," said Ms. Fridge as they huddled up. "Kianna, you've been working hard. You take a rest. Elisha will sub in for you."

The Ravens cheered, the horn sounded and the second quarter started.

"How are you feeling, Jazz?" asked Ms. Fridge.

"Okay, I guess." Karin and Mia weren't the only girls who'd made mistakes in the first quarter. Pretty much every player on both teams had made bad passes, dropped balls, got called for travelling or missed easy shots.

"Good," said Ms. Fridge. "At the next whistle I'm going to sub Hannah off and put you in. Get ready, you are about to begin your career as a Northside Raven for real."

The team hustled out onto the court. Jazz took her place among them. The Ravens had possession, so Elisha took the ball at the sidelines and inbounded it to Karin.

"Thunderbird," Karin said as she took the pass.

Jazz's mind went blank for a moment. Then she remembered that Thunderbird was a baseline play and position four was supposed to take the shot. Jazz knew Mia was four and Jazz was playing position five. But she couldn't remember what she was supposed to do. Did she slide? Screen? Cut?

Plan your movement, Jazz told herself. Think it through.

All around her, girls scrambled into position. Jazz heard the squeak of sneakers on wood as she stood there, frozen in place. She watched as Karin passed the ball to Kianna, who lobbed it to Mia, who was set up three metres from the hoop, waiting for the pass.

Screen! I'm supposed to screen for Mia! Jazz remembered. But by then it was too late.

The Eagle Mountain defender had anticipated the pass. Without Jazz to screen her, she jumped high into the air, intercepted the ball and drove down the court for the easiest layup she would ever get.

"Jazz!" Mia yelled angrily. "Learn the play. It isn't hard!"

"Don't worry about it, Jazz," said Karin. They hurried down the court to inbound the ball. "You'll get it next time."

But that was easier said than done for Jazz. For the next five minutes her ears burned with Mia's words. Karin didn't call Thunderbird again. Eagle Mountain wasn't very strong on defence, so Karin called Raptor three times in a row and went in herself, scoring each time.

On offence and defence, nobody passed Jazz the ball. She touched it just twice. Once was when she got a defensive rebound and passed the ball up to Hannah. The other time wasn't as good. An Eagle Mountain player fumbled the ball. Jazz picked it up and tried to pass it to Mia, the closest Raven to her. But her pass was slow and an Eagle Mountain player quickly stepped in front of Mia and caught the ball.

This time Mia didn't say anything, exactly. Instead, she let out an exaggerated sigh. Jazz knew exactly what it meant. You're no good at this game. You shouldn't be here. That was what Mia was telling her.

A couple of minutes later the Eagle Mountain coach called a time out. Even with Jazz's mistake, the Ravens were winning by ten. They had gone on a six-point run, thanks to Karin and Mia, who hit all their shots.

"I really don't feel good, Coach," Jazz said to Ms. Fridge, what little confidence she had now gone. "I think I'm going to throw up."

"Okay," said Ms. Fridge. "You've done well. Get a drink and have a seat. There's only a couple of minutes left in the third. We should be okay with six players."

Jazz watched the rest of the game from the bench. With five minutes to go, the Northside Ravens were up by six points. A few minutes later, Eagle Mountain had fought their way back so the Ravens were leading by only two. The game was up for grabs when an Eagle Mountain player went up for a jumpshot and missed. Kianna took the rebound and quickly fed the ball to Karin, who passed it to Mia. With thirty seconds left on the clock, Mia pulled up at the three-point line and shot.

The ball arced high into the air and went through the hoop. Nothing but net! The team and the small Ravens crowd cheered as the Ravens went up by five. But not Jazz. Jazz hated Mia more than anything now, especially when Mia flashed Jazz a smile as she ran back to take her position on defence.

Eagle Mountain made one more shot to bring the game within three. But that was as close as they came. The game ended 55–52 for the Ravens. The Ravens gathered for a cheer, shook hands with Eagle Mountain and went into the change room to celebrate.

Everyone but Jazz. She picked up her backpack and walked over to her mom, who had come down to congratulate her.

"You did great, Jazz!" her mom started to say with a big smile. Then she saw Jazz's face and her smile turned into a look of worry. "What's wrong?" she asked. "Don't you want to be in there with your teammates?"

"No," Jazz snapped. "I just want to go home."

11 Practice Makes PERFECT

It took the weekend and a call to Akisha for Jazz to feel better. But once she did, she worked extra hard. Practice was ending when Ms. Fridge called Jazz over. "Can I speak to you for a minute, Jazz?"

"Sure." Jazz felt a little nervous and a little embarrassed about what happened after the game. She had left without joining the team in the change room. She knew Ms. Fridge would talk to her about it.

"You've worked really hard in practice today. I just wanted to let you know I appreciate that. You look like you are feeling better as well. You must have been pretty sick last week. You left right after the game, and I didn't have a chance to talk with you."

"I'm feeling better," was all Jazz said. But she was glad that Ms. Fridge noticed her effort.

"That is great news," said the coach. "We play the Riverwood Rapids Friday afternoon. Exhibition game or not, they're our biggest rivals, you know. We're going to need all hands on deck, as they say. It will be a fast game." Ms. Fridge looked at Jazz closely. "I also wanted to ask if everything was all right. No problems between you and anyone on the team, is there?"

"Not at all," Jazz said quickly. "Why would you think that?"

"Well, it seems to me that there's a little bit of tension between you and Mia. Anything you want to talk about?"

There was a lot Jazz wanted to talk about. But not to Ms. Fridge. She'd called her sister a couple of times and Akisha had told her what to do. Outwork, outhustle, outplay. That was how to get people like Mia to back off. It was good advice and Jazz had taken it to heart. Tattling to her coach wouldn't be of any use. "No, it's all good."

"Glad to hear it," said Ms. Fridge, "but if there was something you needed to let me know, you'd tell me, right? We all have to put personal differences aside and work together if we want to put up a good fight against Riverwood."

There was no way Jazz was going to let Mia get into her head again. The only way to make sure of it was to be better than Mia on the court, outplaying and outworking her. Jazz remembered the things she'd learned in therapy. Think about the movement. Plan it out in your head. Practise it time and time again until it becomes natural.

That was what Jazz did, for hours and hours that week. Raven, Thunderbird, Viking. In her driveway, in her mind and in practice Jazz ran the plays through her head. Plan your movement. Think it through. Practice makes perfect. Jazz had hated therapy, but those simple strategies had been helpful. By the end of the week, Jazz felt sure she would never make a mistake or forget a play ever again. When it came time for the second game of the season, Jazz was nervous, but ready.

The game was an away game at Riverwood Secondary, Northside's biggest rival. Northside's boys teams were usually stronger than Riverwood's, but the Riverwood Rapids girls' program was a three-time provincial championship winner. The previous season, though, the Riverwood senior girls' team had been knocked out of the provincial championship by Northside in the quarter-finals. There was a lot of buzz about the game, even for an exhibition, and the stands were full.

The Ravens did their warm-up, then huddled around Ms. Fridge for last-minute instructions.

"Our first game was good. But there were some sloppy moments," said the coach. "Catch and control, that's the key. Before you pass, before you shoot, before you dribble, make sure you have caught the ball and it is under your control. If it's not, that's when turnovers happen."

"Catch and control," said Karin. "You bet, Coach."

The teammates took their places on the court. The Ravens were in their black-and-red road uniforms,

Riverwood in their home white-and-green ones. Jazz and Kianna started on the bench. But Ms. Fridge had promised they would all see a lot of floor time. This game was going to be fast and tough.

Jazz couldn't wait. She watched in surprise as Hannah won the opening tipoff and tapped the ball to Karin. The Rapids centre was a tall Chinese Canadian girl, easily several centimetres taller than Hannah. Clearly no one on the Rapids team had thought Hannah would win, judging by how flat-footed they were.

Karin found herself wide open. Jazz cheered as Karin sprinted towards the Riverwood net and put a nice layup off the glass for two easy points. With less than ten seconds played in the game, Northside was already winning.

Seven minutes later, Ms. Fridge called a time out. Riverwood had been on a run, scoring eight points in a row. They were leading Northside by four. Number twenty-three, Riverwood's point guard, had got most of the points. She was tiny, but she moved like a cheetah and had an incredible shot.

Just as the coach had predicted, the pace of the game was very fast and the girls were tired.

"Elisha, take a rest. Kianna will take your position. Cerys, you, too. Up you get, Jazz. I need you to hustle out there."

You got this, Jazz said to herself. She hurried onto the court right after Karin led the cheer. She took her position and watched as Mia inbounded the ball to Karin.

"Thunderbird!" Karin shouted.

Plan your movement. Think it through. Thunderbird is a screen and roll play. I set the screen. Jazz remembered right away what she was supposed to do. She got into position and watched as Hannah rolled behind her. The play ran like clockwork. Karin faked, Mia cut in and took a perfect bounce pass. Two steps later she was in the air, putting the ball into the net.

"That's what I'm talking about!" Ms. Fridge yelled excitedly from the sidelines.

A minute later Northside was up by one after Kianna sunk a great three-point shot. But there was no time to celebrate. The girls had to get back on defence.

Ms. Fridge had called for a 2-3 zone defence. Some of the defences were tricky, but Jazz liked zone once she figured it out. It was simple and she didn't have to run all over the place.

Jazz stood on the left side of the key. She bounced on her toes, her arms high and wide. She watched as a Riverwood forward cut through the key. She's getting the pass, Jazz thought. Jazz wasn't sure how she knew it, but she did. Sure enough, the point guard threw the ball to the cutter. Jazz was ready.

Jazz stepped towards the ball and intercepted it, catching it cleanly. She held onto it for just a second before passing to Karin.

"Great job, Jazz!" cheered Karin as the girls moved into their offensive positions.

Karin saw an opening and called Raptor and dribbled in for the layup. But she put the ball on the glass too hard. It rolled around the rim and fell outside the hoop.

Before the ball could hit the ground or end up with a Riverwood defender, Jazz jumped and picked up the rebound. She landed on the floor and pump-faked to throw off the Riverwood player beside her. Then she went back up and scored her first points as a Raven.

Jazz heard her mom cheer in the stands as she hustled back to defence, her heart pounding. Jazz looked at Mia triumphantly. I do have this! she thought. Defence and offence both! Maybe practice does make perfect after all!

12 Catch and CONTROL

With two minutes left in the game, Northside was up 44–41. Jazz had played for most of the game. She'd even scored another three baskets. The only thing that bothered Jazz was that Mia wouldn't pass to her. Even when Jazz was open and could have made an easy basket, Mia took the shot herself or dished it off to someone else. The Ravens could have been up by at least four more points, but Jazz didn't have time to worry about that.

With less than forty seconds left, the Riverwood shooting guard took a shot two metres out from the hoop. She missed, but only because Hannah jumped up and fell into her. The Riverwood player hit the ground hard and the ref blew the whistle. It wasn't on purpose, but an angry cry rose up from the Riverwood fans. There was a lot of history between the schools, and Hannah had a reputation as a tough player.

Hannah leaned over and helped the Riverwood girl to her feet, then walked to the bench. The foul was

Hannah's fifth and final of the game. She'd been like a bull on the court, playing tough. It was no surprise she'd fouled out. Elisha hurried off the bench and took Hannah's position at the top of the key.

Jazz lined up across from Kianna and watched as the Riverwood guard took her first free throw shot. She bounced the ball twice, spun it around in her hands and then shot. The ball arced through the air and fell through the hoop. Swish! The Riverwood fans and bench cheered, then fell silent to wait for the second shot.

Two bounces. A quick spin and she shot again. This time the ball hit the back of the rim, right where it attached to the backboard. Jazz watched, knees bent, ready to jump for the rebound. The ball bounced, rolled around the rim. Then, almost reluctantly, it fell through the net. The Riverwood fans cheered again — 44–43. Northside's lead was now only one point.

Ms. Fridge called a time out. The Ravens hurried to the bench.

"Listen carefully," said Ms. Fridge. "The last thing we need to do is panic. We're up by one and we have the ball. Slow things down, get past half court and keep possession. Catch and control. My bet is that they're going to expect Karin to go in and take the shot herself. So they will be guarding extra close."

That's a safe bet, Jazz thought. Karin had been driving the offence all game.

"Karin," the coach went on, "with five seconds left on the clock I want you to go in and fake the layup. They will try to double- or even triple-team you if they think you're going in for the shot. Mia and Jazz, you've both been having a great game. If Karin can't take the shot, she's going to pass to one of you. Sound good?"

It sounded great to Jazz. With the game on the line, she was being trusted to win for Northside. Jazz had seen her older sister in this situation a hundred times, but she'd never thought she would be in this spot herself.

Ms. Fridge grinned. "Get out there and win this one for the Ravens!"

Elisha inbounded the ball just past half court. Riverwood set up their zone, five girls with their hands up. They looked like a white-and-green wall to Jazz as she stood near the three-point line, waiting for Karin to run the play. Thirty seconds left in the game. Karin was patient, slowly dribbling the ball, looking for her chance. The crowd in the stands was loud, shouting encouragement for Riverwood. Jazz could hardly hear them through the pounding of her heart.

Twenty seconds left. Karin faked to the right and the entire Riverwood defence tilted towards her. She faked to the left, then went back to her right side. Riverwood swarmed Karin, expecting her to drive to the net just like Ms. Fridge had said.

"Now!" Jazz heard Ms. Fridge shout from the bench. Karin took the Riverwood defence farther to the right. It left a gaping hole for Jazz and Mia to fill. Fifteen seconds left in the game.

Ten seconds. Jazz sprinted for the key. Karin saw her coming and lobbed her the ball over the heads of the Riverwood defence. Maybe it was nerves. Maybe it was bad luck. Maybe it was her sweaty hands. Instead of going up and into the open net, the ball slipped out of Jazz's fingers and hit the floor. It rolled right into the hands of a Riverwood player, who scooped it up and ran down the court.

Five seconds. Jazz stood there, her legs frozen. She stared in disbelief as the Riverwood girl went in for the layup. The ball went up against the glass and fell through the hoop. The final buzzer sounded and the home crowd went wild.

Riverwood won 45–44.

The next thing Jazz saw was Mia, standing right in front of her. "You lost us the game!" Mia shouted. "Catch and control! It was the easiest shot in the world. All you had to do was catch it and put it in. But you couldn't even hold onto the stupid ball! You're useless, Jazz! Why'd you even bother trying out? You don't belong here!"

"Mia! That's enough! Line up and shake hands!" Ms. Fridge hurried over to intervene. But by then the damage had been done. All the good feelings, all the confidence Jazz had felt just one minute before was gone. It had slipped from her fingers just like the ball.

For a moment Jazz wished the ground would open up and swallow her. But then, like it came out of nowhere, was anger. Jazz was angrier than she'd ever been in her life.

Before Mia could walk away, Jazz confronted her, her face red, her fists clenched.

"Does it make you feel big to pick on me, Mia? Does it make you feel good to post cruel things online and mock me? I never did anything to you! You are a terrible person! I hate you!"

Mia stood silently. She looked surprised and very uncomfortable as Jazz shouted at her.

"Jazz, step back," Ms. Fridge said. "I'll deal with this." The coach looked worried. Players from both teams stood by nervously, except for Karin, who ran over and put her arm around Jazz. Jazz's mom was hurrying down from the bleachers.

"Everyone says that. But they don't do anything about it, Ms. Fridge. Never!" said Jazz as she stormed away. "I've had enough! I quit!"

13 The Past COMES BACK

Jazz went home and right to her room, too upset to say anything to her mom. How did it go so wrong? she thought. How could she have missed? Jazz knew it was one shot in a game that didn't count for anything. But she still felt as if she'd lost Game Seven of the NBA finals.

Jazz was angry at Mia. But she was angry at herself as well. Angry for missing and angry for agreeing to play in the first place. Then Jazz was sad instead of mad, and after a while she was ashamed of how she'd reacted. Those who know better do better. That was another one of her mom's phrases. Jazz did know better, but that sure hadn't stopped her from blowing up in public.

It was her sister who helped Jazz calm down. Her mom must have let Akisha know what happened. First thing Saturday morning, Jazz's phone rang. For the next hour Akisha and Jazz talked. By the time the conversation ended, Jazz felt much better. Even so,

Jazz didn't feel like seeing or talking to anyone else. She would wait until Monday for that.

***

"Jazz! Why haven't you been answering my calls and messages? I've been worried sick about you!" Karin hurried over to where Jazz was sitting at their usual table in the Commons.

"Hey, Karin," Jazz said. "I'm sorry, I was just trying to figure out things for myself. It took me a while. I felt bad about how I behaved."

"How you behaved? The one who should be embarrassed is Mia," said Karin. "If I was Ms. Fridge, I'd kick Mia off the team, even if that means we are down to six players. I can't believe how horrible she is! You aren't going to quit, though?"

"I don't know." On Friday night, Jazz had been certain she was going to quit the team. But after three days and a long talk with her sister, she wasn't sure anymore. If you quit, you let Mia win. That had been Akisha's advice.

Before Jazz could say anything else, Mia and three of her friends sat down three tables away. If Mia knew Jazz was sitting so close, she didn't show it. Mia and her friends were soon laughing and smiling, looking at something on Mia's phone. Jazz knew it was Mia's because of the bright pink case. She'd seen Mia use it a hundred times before.

"I can't stand Mia," Karin whispered to Jazz. "I'm going to go over there and tell her exactly what I think of her."

"No! Don't!" The last thing Jazz wanted was another scene.

"Are you sure? I really want to give Mia a piece of my mind. She needs to know she can't treat people like that."

"It would only make things worse," said Jazz. "It's not worth it."

"Okay," Karin said. "But only because you are asking, and you are my best friend."

They watched as Mia put her phone down. Mia stood up and walked towards the cafeteria.

"She's getting her lunch," Karin whispered. "I hope she chokes on a hamburger!"

"Karin!" It was a horrible thought, but Jazz couldn't help but laugh.

"No hamburger today," Karin said as the girls saw Mia line up to pay for her food. "Looks like Mia's going for French fries. At the very least, I hope one of the crispy pieces gets stuck in her throat!"

Jazz laughed. Then she noticed she wasn't the only person who found something funny. Back at the table, Mia's friends were huddling around Mia's cell phone, laughing. Just before Mia returned, the girls quickly put her phone down. Mia took her seat and ate her fries.

"Darn!" Jazz said. "She didn't choke."

Karin grinned. "Maybe next time. So what are you going to do, Jazz?"

Jazz had been thinking a lot about that. "I'm not sure. I'm going to go and see Ms. Fridge after school today. I'm not sure she even wants me on the team anymore after my drama. But I owe her an apology for how I acted. It's the least I can do."

Two hours later, Jazz got a message that made her forget all about going to see Ms. Fridge. She was in Ms. Worden's French class when she felt her phone vibrate. Jazz took the phone from her pocket and looked at the screen. The message was from Karin. All it said was, "OMG! BIG NEWS! CYA!"

Karin didn't say anything else. The next twenty minutes of French class dragged and dragged. Finally, the bell rang. Jazz picked up her binder, stuffed it into her backpack and hurried downstairs and out the front door of the school. Karin arrived not one minute later.

"What's up?" Jazz didn't have a clue what had Karin so excited. But she could tell it was something big.

"Elisha was in Social Studies class in Block C with Mia when Ms. Webb came in and took Mia out of the room," Karin explained. "Ms. Webb looked really mad."

"Why? What happened?" Jazz could hardly believe what she was hearing.

"I don't know exactly," Karin said. "But someone saw Mia in Ms. Webb's office with the police. My social media is lighting up. It sounds like Mia made an online threat to somebody at Eagle Mountain. They are taking it very seriously. Mia's in big trouble!"

14 Just What She DESERVES

"Mia's going to get kicked off the team," Karin said. "Maybe even expelled from Northside."

"And arrested, too, I hope," said Jazz.

Both girls laughed the entire walk home. It was a cold day in late November. The leaves had fallen from the trees and frost had stayed on the ground all day. But at least it wasn't raining. The sun shone. After a week of Vancouver rain, the sun lifted Jazz's spirits almost as much as the news about Mia.

Mia's post was all over social media. Somebody had taken a screenshot and shared it. Every student with a phone in the entire school district had seen it. It was terrible what Mia had said. No wonder the police were involved. Many kids at Northside were shocked how cruel the post was. But not Jazz. Mia had bullied Jazz online in elementary school. Now she had done it to some poor girl at Eagle Mountain, but even worse. Finally, Mia was going to get what she deserved.

"So when are you going to talk to Ms. Fridge?" Karin asked when they reached Jazz's house. "You have no reason to leave the team now. Mia will be kicked off for sure."

Jazz groaned. "Ms. Fridge! I can't believe I forgot to see her!" Jazz had intended to see the coach after school, but with all the excitement around Mia it had slipped her mind. Maybe it was a good thing she hadn't gone see the coach. At lunch, Jazz had been unsure about what she was going to do, but she had no doubt anymore. Now Jazz would stay and play with the other five girls. It didn't matter if they won a single game. Things would be better with Mia gone.

"I'll email her tonight," said Jazz. "I won't quit, Karin. I promise."

Jazz went straight to the garage, put down her backpack and picked up her ball. Her mom was at work and wouldn't be home for an hour. She wanted to shoot, to practise layups and three-point shots, until then. Plan your movement. Think it through. Practise. Catch and control. Jazz ran through the plays until she could do them in her sleep. Jazz was tired but happy when her mom pulled into the driveway.

"It's good to see you with a basketball in your hand, Jazz," said her mom, getting out of the car. "I wasn't sure you would pick up one again after last week. How was your day?"

"Best day ever, Mom," said Jazz. She put down the ball and hugged her mother.

★★★

"You're sure about this?" her mom asked when Jazz told her what had happened. "Mia's kicked out of school?"

"Well, not for sure," said Jazz. "But I know she was in Ms. Webb's office and that the police were there. I also saw what she posted."

"You don't know this poor girl, do you? The one at the other school?"

"No," Jazz replied. "I've never heard of her."

"Then how could you have seen the post?"

"Are you kidding me, Mom? You know how social media works, right? Hundreds of people have seen the post. Thousands. It's in group chats all over the place. I wouldn't be surprised if Mia had to leave town. A lot of people are very angry with her."

"You don't have a copy saved in your phone, do you? I don't want you keeping such trash, Jaspreet." Her mom asked the question in Punjabi, a sign she wasn't pleased.

"Of course not, Mom. I promise. Would you like to check my phone?" Jazz wasn't lying, but she wasn't telling the whole truth either. Jazz had seen the screenshot but had deleted the picture almost at once.

Jazz knew her mom had Jazz's password and checked her social media from time to time. Jazz didn't like it, but her mom was old school when it came to things like that. Since her mom paid her phone bill, it wasn't like Jazz could say no.

"If you say you don't, then I believe you, Jazz," her mom said. "But I'm a little disappointed how much you are enjoying the situation Mia finds herself in."

Jazz could hardly believe it. "Why? You know what a terrible person she is! I hope she gets kicked out of school and goes to jail. She's been so mean to so many people, it's the least she deserves."

"I don't disagree that Mia has been very cruel to you. And she's caused a great deal of hurt," her mother said. "But those who know better —"

"Mom!" Jazz cut off her mom before she could finish the sentence. "I don't need to do better. Mia does. She's the one who got herself in big trouble online. Again."

"You're right. Mia seems to have done this to herself. All I'm saying is that gloating over someone's misfortune, no matter how much you dislike them, is beneath you. You're better than that. Anyway, enough about Mia. Time to eat."

After dinner, Jazz helped her mom clean up. Then she excused herself and went to her room. She had Math and French homework, and wanted to do as well as possible. Jazz had been surprised she'd made the honour roll the first term of the semester. For the first time in her life, she felt smart in school. She wanted to do even better in the second term.

Jazz emailed Ms. Fridge. She apologized for how she had acted after the game and told her she would be at practice tomorrow. Then Jazz studied.

At 9:30, Jazz turned off her computer. She needed a good night's sleep. She would work harder than ever at practice. Mia would be kicked off the Ravens. With only six girls on the team, Jazz would be seeing a lot of court time. Jazz sent a quick message to Karin to say goodnight, then climbed into bed.

Jazz was a little mad at her mom. Those who know better do better. Gloating is beneath you. Was Jazz happy that Mia was in trouble? Absolutely, but that wasn't Jazz's fault. Mia was a bad person who did bad things. She deserved to be punished. No matter what her mom said, it felt good to enjoy Mia's misfortune. Jazz was going to gloat. Just a little bit.

15 Innocent Until PROVEN GUILTY

Jazz knew it was going to be a great day at school. The police and the school principal would be looking into the matter. Mia would be suspended and then kicked out of Northside, for sure. No more Mia in the Commons. No more Mia on the team. Jazz wasn't going to quit basketball after all. It didn't matter if they won a single game all season, everything would be fine if Mia was gone.

"She's finally getting what she deserves," said Jazz. She was walking into the school with Karin. "All the mean stuff she pulled in the past has come back to . . ."

Jazz stopped short. She could see Mia inside the school office, sitting with her mom and dad. Mia looked like she'd been crying. Jazz stood and watched as Ms. Webb walked up to them and waved them into her office.

Jazz could hardly believe her eyes. "Why is Mia still here?"

"I don't know," Karin said. "Maybe Ms. Webb is kicking her out right now and is giving her parents the news."

"I hope so," Jazz replied. "I really do."

But at lunch, Mia was still in the school. Jazz watched Mia walk out of the Commons by herself. Mia's usual friends were nowhere to be seen. Other students looked at Mia and laughed.

"I can't believe she's still a student here," said Jazz, shocked for the second time that day.

"Maybe Ms. Webb and the police are investigating," Karin said. "Maybe her parents begged for her to stay until it's done. You know — innocent until proven guilty, that sort of thing."

"She's not innocent of anything," Jazz said. "She's getting what she deserves."

"You don't know the half of it," said Karin. "My social media is lighting up. Look at this!"

Karin gave Jazz her phone. Jazz read through one of the grade eight group chats. It was full of nasty comments and even meaner memes.

"That one's pretty good," said Jazz. It was a meme of Mia behind bars with a cruel comment underneath it.

"Mia's gone viral," said Karin. "And not for anything good. I almost feel sorry for her. Nothing Ms. Webb or the police could do would be worse than what's happening online."

"I don't feel sorry for Mia," Jazz replied. "Not one bit. She's finally getting a taste of her own medicine."

The day finally ended and Jazz hurried to the gym for practice. Practice today, practice tomorrow.

And then the first real game of the season against Riverwood. When Jazz walked into the gym she saw only Ms. Fridge and five other girls.

"No Mia. Win–win," said Karin as they stretched. "Looks like she was guilty as charged. Six players or not, we are better off without her."

Then, for the third time that day, Jazz was shocked. Mia walked out of the change room and onto the floor. The team fell silent. All the girls were looking at Mia. None were happy to see her.

"I didn't do it," was all Mia said. She looked upset and not her usual arrogant self.

"Like you didn't in elementary school?" It was Karin who said it. But judging by the nods and comments, the other girls on the team didn't believe Mia either.

"That's enough," said Ms. Fridge. "We all know there's been a bit of excitement off the court recently. We don't need any of it on the court."

Excitement wasn't exactly the word Jazz would have used. Anger and drama for sure, but not excitement.

"Your job as a team," said Ms. Fridge, "all seven of you — is to pull together. I need you to practise hard and get ready to play Riverwood in the first game of the season tomorrow. Now, everyone get a ball and line up in front of the cones on the floor. Right-hand dribble first two times through, then left hand, then crossovers. Take a shot when you clear the cones. Let's see if we can get ten in a row."

Doing her best to forget that Mia was on the court instead of being expelled, Jazz picked up a ball. Dribbling was a skill Jazz had worked hard on. It looked easy enough on TV when Kyle Lowry or LeBron James moved down the court at top speed. But when you had a condition that affected your coordination, it took a lot of practice and concentration.

The purpose of the drill was to dribble down the court over the cones, without the ball touching them. Every step, every dribble had to be perfect or the ball would hit a cone and send it flying.

Karin led off, moving seamlessly down the row of cones. She didn't disturb a single one. At the end of the row, she went in for a layup. But instead of just putting it off the glass, Karin reversed sides and spun. The ball dropped into the hoop. Karin picked it up and ran down the court to get back in line. She shot Mia a look as she ran past.

Then it was Mia's turn. Like Karin, she dribbled through the cones without touching one. When she was clear, she pivoted quickly to the right. Then out to the three-point line and she launched the ball. Swish! The shot was perfect. Mia grabbed her ball and hurried back, not making any eye contact with the other players.

Jazz started down the cones. Plan your movement. Think it through. Catch and control. The ball went down to the floor then back to her hand as she picked up speed. It bounced again, landing in the area between the cones. Jazz was through. She breathed a sigh of relief, then went in for a simple layup.

Soon all the players were through. No one disturbed a single cone, although Hannah missed her shot. They did right hand again, and Jazz felt her confidence building as she picked up speed. Then it was left-handed. This was harder for Jazz. She hit a cone. But she made up for it by making a nice jumpshot two metres out from the hoop.

Jazz didn't hit another cone, even when she did the crossover dribble, pushing the ball from her right hand to her left. This was one of the skills she'd practised for hours in her driveway. In darkness, the hoop lit up by the front porch light. The time she had put in was paying off and Jazz knew it. She felt better and better every time she ran through the cones, even with Mia on the court.

"Get some water, then let's run our offences," said Ms. Fridge.

Jazz took a quick drink from her water bottle and hurried back onto the court.

"We'll start with Thunderbird," said the coach. "Elisha and Hannah, play defence for the first little bit. I know it's five on two, but I don't want you to let anyone score, okay?"

"You bet, Coach!" Hannah was the most competitive player on the team. Jazz knew that she would play hard to prevent a basket — practice or not. Hannah and Elisha had placed themselves in a simple two-person zone under the hoop. They were bouncing on their toes, ready for the challenge.

"Thunderbird!" said Karin as the team ran into position.

Jazz ran to set the screen. Mia rolled behind her as Karin dribbled into the offensive zone. Hannah and Elisha were playing like they were three metres tall. Karin head faked, she bobbed and cut back and forth. But she couldn't find an opening until Mia cut back into the key.

Karin saw the chance and passed. But before Mia could go up for the shot, Hannah was all over her. Jazz moved to the side and Mia bounce-passed the ball out to her. The key was jammed with players and there was no way Jazz could go in for a layup. So she squared up and shot, a beautiful jumpshot just inside the three-point line. The ball bounced once on the rim then fell through.

"Great shot, Jazz! And great pass, Mia!" said Ms. Fridge. "Let's run it again. If we can play like that against Riverwood tomorrow, we just might have a chance!"

16 A Stray THOUGHT

"Can you believe the nerve of Mia?" said Karin as they walked home from school.

"Actually coming to practice!"

"'I didn't do it'!" laughed Jazz, mimicking Mia. "Who does she think she's fooling?"

"Not us and hopefully not Ms. Webb," said Karin. "Ms. Webb had better do the right thing and kick Mia out by tomorrow. We shouldn't have to put up with her for another minute. Let alone have to play with her."

"Can I see Mia's post again?" asked Jazz. Karin passed over the phone and Jazz looked at the post. "How can Mia say she didn't do it? It's from her account. You can see her name. You can even see the time-stamp. She made the post yesterday at lunch."

"Maybe that's what her friends were laughing at when they picked up her phone," said Karin. "Remember?"

I didn't do it. Mia had sounded sincere. Then an uncomfortable thought hit Jazz. "Or maybe one of them made the post, Karin. They put her phone down right before she got back with her fries."

"Get real, Jazz! Those girls aren't the nicest people in the school. But that online stuff is all Mia."

"You're probably right," Jazz agreed. "Ms. Webb will find out Mia is guilty. Mia will be gone by tomorrow morning."

"You bet," Karin said. "Mia kicked out of school and our first game of the season. I think tomorrow is going to be the best day of the year!"

But the next day didn't start how Jazz had hoped. Mia was still in school. Like Jazz, Karin and the other girls on the team, Mia was wearing the Ravens track suit. It was a sure sign she was going to play.

Jazz couldn't believe what she saw. "What is Ms. Webb doing? How much proof does a person need?"

"Ms. Webb isn't the only one Mia needs to worry about," said Karin. "Have you seen what people are saying about her online now? She's being trolled pretty bad."

Jazz had seen. Someone at Eagle Mountain had started an online petition demanding Mia be kicked out of the entire school district. Hundreds of people had liked it, adding comments of their own. The group chats were full of nasty comments and the memes had gotten worse.

"She has it coming," Jazz said, but she wasn't so sure any more. Even she was starting to feel a little sorry for Mia. Jazz knew what it was like to be bullied online. Whether Mia deserved the attacks or not, Jazz knew all too well how awful it felt to be targeted like that.

"Hopefully today's the last time we have to play with her," said Karin. "We may be stuck with Mia today. But surely Ms. Webb and the police will have this dealt with tomorrow. I hope Mia enjoys the game. It will be the last time she ever wears a Ravens jersey."

17 The Season STARTS

Jazz didn't feel the butterflies in her stomach until she walked out of the change room. There were at least two hundred people sitting in the bleachers. They were all waiting to see the Northside Ravens Grade Eight girls' basketball team start their season for real.

Jazz heard a familiar voice cheering. She looked up to see her mom waving her Ravens flag, the same flag she had when Akisha won the provincials almost nine months before. Jazz could hardly believe that it was her, not her sister, playing now.

Loud music pumped from the gym's speakers. The girls warmed up, running passes, shooting and dribbling as the clock ticked down to game time. Mia was there as well, running the warm-ups. None of the girls spoke to her.

The horn sounded and both teams hurried to their benches.

"Okay, Northside," said Ms. Fridge. "We are going to have to play tough, but also smart. They have a much deeper bench than we do. We can't let them tire us out. We have to play as a team. All of us together. Am I clear?"

Jazz knew what Ms. Fridge meant. Mia was still on the team and would be treated like everyone else. The off-court drama had to be put aside — for now.

"Set up your plays and execute them well," the coach continued. "We will run a 2-3 zone on defence. Hands up and play tough. Cerys and Kianna will start on the bench. The rest of you, get out there and take your positions. And watch the fouls. We need everyone to last the whole game. That means you, Hannah."

"I'll be nice," said Hannah. "I promise." Everyone knew that if anyone on the team was likely to get into foul trouble, it was Hannah. She was one of the nicest, most even-tempered people off the court. On the court? That was something else entirely.

The crowd cheered when the team took their spots on the court. Jazz looked to the bleachers. She saw her mom holding up her phone so Akisha could watch through FaceTime. Jazz looked at the banners hanging on the wall, then at the number seven on the front of her jersey. Jazz wanted to win the game more than anything.

The centres lined up, eight players circling around them. The ref tossed the ball high into the air between Hannah and the tall Riverwood centre with short hair. Hannah leaped and flicked the ball behind her to Mia.

Mia quickly passed to Karin, and the Northside Ravens hustled into their offensive positions. The rest of the team might hate Mia, but she was on the team for now.

"Raptor!" shouted Karin. The Ravens had moved quicker than the Riverwood Rapids had expected and only two Rapids players were set up on defence. Jazz and the other girls ran towards the key to set up for a rebound as Karin dribbled. Karin head faked left, completely fooling the Rapids defender. She went in for the layup — 2–0 Ravens!

A minute later it was 5–0 for the Ravens after Mia robbed a Rapids player of the ball and was fouled when she went in for her own shot. Despite being roughed up, Mia made the basket and the foul shot after. The home crowd cheered madly.

Two minutes later, the Rapids scored a great three-point shot, then stole the ball from Hannah in the Ravens' backcourt. Hannah tried to recover the ball, but hit the Rapids player as she went up for the shot. The Rapids player missed, but went two for two on the line. What hurt worse than the two points was that Hannah, the toughest Ravens defender, took a foul.

On their next play, the Rapids picked up a defensive rebound when Karin missed a three-point shot. The Rapids rebounder quickly fed the ball up the court. Jazz watched in frustration as number five on the Rapids hit a nice jumpshot. The game had started

5–0 for Northside. But now they were losing by two, thanks to a Riverwood seven-point run.

Ms. Fridge called a time out to settle the team. "Slow it down. There's lots of time left in the game. If you keep playing like this, you won't make it to halftime."

Karin called the play as soon as the ball was inbounded. "Thunderbird!"

Mia ran down to set the screen and Jazz took up her position near the baseline. Karin pretended to go in for the layup, but sent a perfect bounce pass to Jazz. Catch and control.

The ball hit Jazz's hands. She squeezed tight, making sure that she had it. Then she jumped up, laying the ball cleanly off the glass. Jazz watched as the ball dropped through the hoop, hardly believing she had scored in a real game.

Thirty seconds later, Riverwood went up by three. Number twenty-three, Riverwood's lightning-quick point guard, drove towards the Ravens' basket. She went right into Hannah on her way to the hoop. Jazz was sure she would get called for an offensive charge. But to everyone's surprise, the ref called a blocking foul on Hannah. That gave Hannah her two fouls before the end of the first quarter.

For the next three minutes, the game went back and forth. Karin sank a beautiful three-point shot to tie the game 10–10. But Riverwood responded with two three-point shots of their own, one right after the other.

Jazz pulled the Ravens to within four points just before the quarter ended. Mia had gone in for a shot that just missed. The ball rolled around the rim then dropped right into Jazz's hands. Despite being surrounded by three Rapids defenders, Jazz went up and dropped the ball through the hoop just as the buzzer sounded to end the quarter.

Riverwood 16, Northside 12.

"Only four points down," said Karin as the team huddled up. "We can do this! We really can!"

18 Jazz Gets a SCARE

Halfway through the second quarter, Riverwood's dangerous number twenty-three point guard had the ball. Hannah reached in to try to steal it. She intended to get the ball, but instead she slapped the guard's hand loud enough to hear from the bench.

"No!" cried Hannah in frustration. The ref blew the whistle and called her third foul of the game.

"Jazz, go in for Hannah," said Ms. Fridge.

Hannah took her seat on the bench, clearly upset with herself. Riverwood was up by six points again. It was 18–12, with five minutes to go before halftime.

A few seconds after Jazz subbed in, Kianna hit a great three-point shot, pulling the Ravens within three. But Riverwood extended their lead by two when their tall centre jumped high into the air on a Riverwood offensive rebound and tapped the ball into the net — 20–15 for Riverwood.

The Riverwood coach started subbing her starters off the floor to give them a rest. It was an option

Ms. Fridge did not have. Jazz's legs grew heavy and her breath came in ragged gasps. Hannah was in foul trouble and Ms. Fridge kept her on the bench, which meant the Ravens had only one sub. When the horn sounded and the first half of the game ended, Jazz could hardly believe that the Rapids were only up 24–20.

The exhausted team followed Ms. Fridge to the change room. Jazz groaned as she lay on a bench, her entire body hurting.

"Rest up for five minutes," said their coach. "Drink water and prepare yourself for the second half."

The fifteen-minute break between halves went very quickly. Jazz and the rest of the team walked back on the court. The Ravens faced the Rapids starters, including their point guard and centre.

Riverwood had possession and, when the ref blew the whistle, they quickly inbounded down the court into Ravens territory.

Slow it down, Ms. Fridge had said in the brief huddle before the game restarted. Control the game.

Hannah was back on the court while Mia and Kianna started on the bench. All the girls would be playing hard for the final sixteen minutes. They would need as much rest as possible.

"Raptor!" Karin cried as she drove down the court. Riverwood was out of position and Karin took advantage, streaking towards the net. Nobody could catch her and she hit the easy layup. The crowd went wild as Northside pulled within one basket of the Rapids. Even though they had a smaller, shorter team, the Ravens were hanging in.

Then disaster struck. Karin pulled up for a three-point shot. The ball hit the back of the rim and bounced high into the air. Jazz jumped up, fighting for the rebound. She caught the ball but landed awkwardly and off balance. As soon as Jazz hit the court, she felt a sharp, stabbing pain in her ankle.

Jazz fell to the floor. She sat there, grimacing in pain, her hands on her ankle. The ref blew the whistle to stop play.

"Are you okay?"

Jazz looked up from the floor. Jazz was surprised to see Mia standing over her, looking worried.

Before Jazz could answer, Ms. Fridge hurried onto the court, as did Ms. Yao from the stands. The players moved back to give Jazz and the coaches space, all except Karin, who stayed beside her friend.

"I don't think it's broken, Jazz," said Ms. Yao, looking at Jazz's ankle. "But it might be badly sprained. We're going to help you to the bench and take a closer look. Are you ready?"

Her arms wrapped around Ms. Fridge's and Ms. Yao's shoulders, Jazz slowly got to her feet. With their help, she hopped to the bench as all the players and the crowd clapped to support her.

"Lie down behind the bench," said Ms. Yao. "I need to take off your shoe and look at your ankle."

It was hard, but Jazz did as she was told. She held back the tears as Ms. Yao unlaced her shoe.

"Kianna, can you run and get some ice from the freezer in the PE office, please?"

Kianna hurried off the bench to get the ice for Ms. Yao. She was back within a minute with a full bag. Jazz felt the shock of the ice cubes on her ankle. She also felt the pain lessen right away.

"Definitely not broken," said Ms. Yao as she inspected Jazz's ankle. "You haven't torn anything either. You hyperextended when you rolled on it. But I don't think you've done anything serious. It will be sore for a while, but you should be okay. You got off lucky, Jazz."

"Can I play?" Jazz asked. She felt helpless and wanted to help her team stay in the game.

"I don't know about that," said Ms. Fridge. "I don't want to risk your health."

A part of Jazz agreed with her coach. And she knew her mom was watching anxiously in the bleachers. But first game or last game, this was very important.

"Let me wrap it," said Ms. Yao. "We'll see how she feels by the end of the quarter. I'm not making any promises, Jazz. But I think you got a scare more than you did an injury. Give yourself fifteen minutes to rest. It will be Ms. Fridge's call to let you go in or not."

Last Pick

Jazz stayed on the ground as Ms. Yao wrapped the ice around her ankle with a Tensor bandage. When she was done, Jazz sat up and leaned against the gym wall. She looked up to the stands and gave her mom a thumbs-up. Jazz's mom smiled back. Jazz could see the relief on her face.

Jazz watched from the floor as the two teams went back and forth. Jazz cheered as the Ravens hung in against the bigger team. But no matter what Northside did, Riverwood always managed to stay four to six points ahead.

The Ravens were getting tired and it showed as the play got chippy. Elisha, Mia and even Karin had picked up two fouls each in the third quarter, and Hannah had got her fourth. The Rapids were soon in bonus penalty territory, shooting free throws each time a Ravens player fouled them and not just in the act of shooting. With one minute to go in the third, Riverwood was up by nine, 32–23. The game was slipping out of reach.

Jazz felt her ankle. It was cold and a little tender. But it was nowhere near as bad as it had been when she fell. She said, "Ms. Fridge, I think I'm good to play."

"Let me check," said Ms. Yao. She had stayed on the bench after wrapping Jazz's ankle. "Tell me how it feels. And be honest, Jazz." Ms. Yao unwrapped the bandage.

Jazz gently rolled her foot. "It feels okay."

"Stand up and see if you can put some pressure on it," said Ms. Yao. "It's not swollen, so that's a good sign."

Jazz did as she was asked. Her ankle ached, but it didn't hurt to stand on it.

"Walk a few feet and come back," said Ms. Yao.

Again, Jazz did as she was asked. "It hurts a bit," she said. "But I'm not limping. I can play. Really."

Ms. Yao looked at Ms. Fridge. "Your player, your call, Coach," she said. "But I think Jazz is right. I can tape it up to give her some support if you want her to play."

"You start on the bench, Jazz," said Ms. Fridge after a very long silence. "I want you to rest up some more. And if I put you in, the second your ankle hurts you let me know. No game is worth getting badly hurt. Agreed?"

"Agreed," said Jazz.

The horn sounded. "Then get your shoe back on. The third quarter just ended. We have eight minutes to score ten points and win this thing."

19 Foul TROUBLE

Two minutes into the last quarter, the Northside Ravens were losing by just three points.

Northside had started with the ball and Karin sank a three-pointer. Riverwood had missed on their possession. Karin had picked up the rebound, ran the length of the court, made the layup and was fouled. She had sunk the extra point — 32–29 Riverwood. The crowd had gone wild.

Then Hannah fouled out. She went in for a layup and ploughed right into a Riverwood defender. Hannah stormed to the bench, tears of frustration in her eyes. The whole team was unsettled and Ms. Fridge called a time out.

"Take Hannah's position, Jazz," said Ms. Fridge. "And as soon as your ankle hurts you let me know. I'm not going to have you miss the rest of the season with an injury."

"I promise," said Jazz. She bounced lightly on her foot. Ms. Yao had taped her ankle tightly, and her motion was limited. It felt a little bit like she was wearing a ski boot. But it didn't hurt.

Mia inbounded the ball to Karin.

"Thunderbird!" Karin said as she crossed centre court. She started the play, faking to the left and driving to the right. Jazz took her position on the screen as Elisha ran behind her.

Karin had run the play to perfection. Riverwood fell for the fake, leaving Kianna wide open under the basket. Karin fed the ball to her and Kianna went up for the easiest two points she would ever get — 32–31 Riverwood! The Ravens now trailed by only one point.

A minute later, the Riverwood Rapids centre hit a beautiful three-point shot from the corner. On the next Ravens offensive play, Elisha missed the shot. A Riverwood player picked up the rebound and threw the ball down the court to their guard, who went in for another two points — 37–31 Riverwood.

With four minutes left, Karin shouted, "Viking!" She fed the ball to Mia, who stood at the top of the key. Mia went up and shot. The ball bounced high on the front of the rim. Jazz watched as it hung there in mid-air before falling through the hoop for three points — 37–34 Riverwood.

Jazz's ankle had started to throb. But the last thing she was going to do was ask to be subbed off. With three minutes left, taking a break wasn't an option.

Especially since Elisha picked up her fifth and final foul. She had reached in for the ball and missed, her hand landing on the Riverwood player's arm.

With two minutes left, the Ravens got a lucky break when the Riverwood point guard missed a shot. Mia picked up the rebound and gave it to Karin.

"Thunderbird!" Karin shouted.

Jazz set the screen and Karin tried to fake, but Riverwood didn't bite. Instead they closed in on Karin. With no options, Karin threw the ball blindly towards the net. The ball bounced on the rim several times and somehow it fell through the hoop — 37–36 Riverwood! The crowd was going crazy.

Jazz looked at Karin and smiled. Karin shrugged her shoulders, not believing herself that she had made the shot.

The Riverwood coach called a time out. Her team had seen a nine-point lead shrink to one. The Rapids looked rattled.

Ms. Fridge looked at Jazz. "How's your ankle?" she asked.

"I'm fine," said Jazz. At this point Jazz wasn't going to say anything different.

The horn sounded. The Ravens cheered and took their positions on defence. Riverwood's point guard faked a pass, then darted into the top of the key and shot. Jazz watched as the ball arced high into the air, certain it would be good. But the ball landed short and hit the front of the rim. It bounced right to Cerys, who grabbed it and held on tightly until Mia got open and took the pass.

Mia fed the ball back to Karin. The Ravens went on offence with one minute left on the clock.

"Raptor!"

Karin sped towards the Rapids net. She went in and put the ball neatly against the glass. But instead of dropping through the hoop like it had done a hundred times before, the ball rolled around. It fell out. The fans groaned. What could have been the game-winning shot landed in the hands of the Riverwood centre.

The whistle blew again as Riverwood called their last time out. Fifty seconds left to play.

"They are going to run the shot clock down," said Ms. Fridge. "But they have to shoot. We should have one possession left, even if they score. Play tough defence. But no fouls, no matter what. If they score, I'll call a time out. If they don't, you have twenty seconds to run a play. Karin, I want you to take the shot if you can."

"Got it, Coach," said Karin. If she was mad at herself for missing the easy layup it didn't show. Jazz admired her friend for her perseverance.

The horn sounded again.

"Win or lose, I'm proud of all of you," said Ms. Fridge. "I really am."

"Go, Ravens!" Karin led the cheer and the Ravens took their positions.

Last Pick

Jazz felt her heart pounding as she stood at the top of the key. Her hands were raised, her eyes locked on the Riverwood player inbounding the ball.

Jazz watched the numbers tick away: 49, 48, 47. The Riverwood point guard dribbled slowly between the top of the key and centre court. The Ravens held their places as the other four Rapids players moved quickly around the court. They darted everywhere, looking for an opening, trying to draw the Ravens out of position.

With ten seconds left on the shot clock and thirty seconds left in the game, Riverwood made their move. Their tall centre darted through the key. Their point guard moved as if she was going to lob it in. The Ravens zone collapsed as they moved to cover. But instead of passing, the Rapids point guard put her head down and dribbled, taking the ball to the hoop herself. She pulled up three metres from the hoop and shot.

Jazz held her breath as the ball cut through the air. It landed on the left side of the rim, bounced up against the glass, hit the rim again. Then it rolled along the front of the orange metal, moving slowly, as if it wasn't sure where it wanted to go.

Twenty-five seconds to go. Twenty-four. The ball rolled and dropped outside the hoop. The ball bounced and rolled in the key, loose right under the Riverwood net. Jazz moved first. She dove for the ball and reached it a split second before the Riverwood centre. Too off balance to grab it, Jazz did the only thing she could. She punched at the ball, sending it flying right to Kianna. Kianna quickly threw it to Karin, who was standing by herself near centre court. Surrounded by a sea of legs, Jazz couldn't see Karin streak down the court, couldn't see her go in for the layup. But she knew her friend had scored by the great cheer that came up from the crowd — 38–37 Northside!

Cerys and Mia helped Jazz to her feet and the girls set up again on defence. Riverwood had no more time outs and would have to inbound the ball at the far end of the court. Northside was up by one, but the Riverwood Rapids had twenty seconds left to make a play. It was more than enough time to score.

"No fouls!" shouted Ms. Fridge from the bench.

Jazz watched as number twenty-three, the Riverwood point guard, crossed centre court. The rest of the Rapids buzzed like a swarm of wasps, looking for an opening. The time ticked down — 18, 17, 16, second after second disappearing.

The Rapids centre cut through the key. This time, the point guard fed her the ball. Jazz held her position. The centre caught the ball and went up for the shot, pressing against Jazz as she did. Jazz stood still, arms raised high.

Five seconds left. Jazz felt the centre make contact. She was terrified the ref would call her for a foul. But the whistle didn't tweet. The only thing Jazz heard was the sound of the ball bouncing on the rim and the roar of the crowd when Mia jumped and caught the rebound. Mia held onto the ball, cradling it in her arms, bending over to protect it. One second left. Riverwood swatted at the ball, trying to knock it free.

No seconds left. The horn sounded, ending the game — 38–37 Northside! The crowd was going crazy.

Jazz could see red marks on Mia's arms. She had been hit over and over as the Rapids had tried to get the ball.

"We won!" said Karin as she hugged Jazz. "I can't believe we won!"

"You played really well, Mia," Jazz said, forgetting for just a second how angry she was with her old enemy. Like her or not, Mia was a major part of their win. She had taken a real beating holding onto the rebound.

"Thanks," Mia said. "You played great, too. How's your ankle?"

"It should be fine," said Jazz.

As the team gathered for a victory cheer, Jazz was still surprised that Mia seemed honestly concerned about her. It's almost a shame that the first game against Riverwood is Mia's last, thought Jazz. She hated Mia more than anything, but she sure could play.

20 Thinking Things THROUGH

Jazz turned off her bedside light then shut her eyes. She was tired from the game and was almost asleep when she heard it. Listen to the little voice inside your head. From out of nowhere it came, and Jazz heard it loud and clear. There was something that wasn't sitting right.

I didn't do it. Mia was a terrible person and a liar. Jazz wanted her gone from her life. But she was having the slightest of doubts. She also felt bad for Mia. Almost. She may have brought it on herself, but Mia had been ripped to pieces online. Jazz knew exactly how that felt and didn't wish it on anyone. Not even Mia.

Listen to the little voice. It will tell you to do the right thing.

Jazz groaned as she tossed and turned. That stupid little voice was telling her to do something tomorrow. She hoped the little voice was wrong. It took Jazz ages to fall asleep.

★★★

"Can I see Mia's post again?" Jazz asked Karin as they walked to school.

"You should just keep a copy," said Karin. She passed her phone over.

Jazz looked, but this time she wasn't looking at what Mia said. Instead, she checked when she had said it. "The time-stamp, Karin. Look at it. I'm pretty sure the post was made when Mia was in line getting food."

"Are you still thinking about that?" her friend asked in disbelief. "Let it go, Jazz! Mia is guilty! I can't believe that you, of all people, are trying to defend her."

"I'm not saying she didn't do it," Jazz insisted. "But —"

"But nothing," Karin cut her off. "Mia did it. Case closed. You know her history better than anyone."

"That's true," Jazz said. "But still, maybe I should say something to Ms. Webb, that's all."

"Jazz, you don't need to say anything. Even if there is a tiny chance Mia didn't do it, you don't owe her anything. You don't have to say a thing. Nobody would know. Forget about it."

The bell rang and Jazz said goodbye to her friend. But I would know, Jazz thought as she walked to class.

The rest of the day went slowly for Jazz. She liked Mr. Williams, her English teacher, but Jazz only half-paid attention to the lesson on poetry. She was distracted in Mr. Estabrook's Home Economics class as well, and nearly burned the bannock they were making. It was a good thing class ended when it did or the whole school could have ended up in flames.

"Nobody's seen Mia today," said Karin to Jazz. They were sitting at their usual place in the Commons for lunch. "I told you she was guilty as charged."

"Probably," agreed Jazz.

"You haven't said anything to anyone about your crazy theory have you?"

"No. Maybe you're right." Jazz hadn't said anything. But she had been thinking about Mia all morning. "Can we talk about something not related to Mia? I'm sick of hearing her name."

"On that I agree completely," said Karin. For the rest of lunch, Karin and Jazz talked about basketball and other gossip. When the bell rang, they went to their afternoon classes.

Math and French classes were even slower for Jazz, despite Mr. Leitch cracking his jokes. All that Jazz could think about was Mia. Mia was definitely not at school, and had probably been expelled. *Mia is guilty and she is getting what she deserves*, thought Jazz. She told herself that about a thousand times.

Then, with ten minutes left until the end of the day, Jazz heard it again. *Listen to the little voice. It will tell you to do the right thing.*

Jazz groaned. It had been whispering to her the entire day, though she had done her best to ignore it. Jazz also knew that there was only one thing she could do to make the stupid thing shut up. So, instead of meeting Karin in the Commons after school, she walked down to the counselling offices.

"Jazz, what a pleasant surprise," said Ms. Yao when Jazz walked in. "How's your ankle?"

"Fine," she said. "Thanks for taping it." Then Jazz took a deep breath.

"What's up?" asked Ms. Yao.

"Mia's been expelled, hasn't she? Because of that online thing."

"I can't talk about other students, Jazz," said Ms. Yao. "But I'm sure there is a lot of gossip out there."

"I know what people are saying, Ms. Yao. I've seen the post."

"But?" It was as if Ms. Yao sensed Jazz was about to say something.

Jazz took a deep breath. "She probably made it. She's done it before. But there is a chance, a small chance, that Mia didn't."

"What do you mean?" Ms. Yao looked very interested in what Jazz was about to say.

"I was having lunch with Karin in the Commons on the day the post was made," Jazz explained. "Mia got up to get food and left her phone on the table. One of her friends picked it up when Mia was in line.

All the girls laughed like it was the funniest thing in the world. Then they put down the phone before Mia came back."

"You're certain about this, Jazz?" asked the counsellor, sounding very serious. "Your elementary school counsellor told me about the history between you and Mia. That's why she's not in any of your classes. I made sure of it when I created your timetable."

"You did?" Jazz had thought it was just luck she wasn't in the same class as Mia for any of her subjects.

"Yes," replied Ms. Yao. "I wanted to give you a good start in high school. I must admit I was surprised to see you both on the basketball team together. I'd hoped that things were better. But, given what Ms. Fridge told me about you getting upset at a practice, I guess that wasn't the case."

"No kidding," said Jazz.

"So even with your history with Mia and after what happened back then, you are coming to Mia's defence?"

"I don't like Mia one bit," Jazz admitted. "Part of me hopes she did it, it really does. I'd feel a lot better if she got expelled but . . ." Jazz left the rest of the sentence unsaid.

Ms. Yao nodded her head. "I understand. You are a very good person, Jazz Sidhu."

The bell rang.

"What now?" asked Jazz.

"Now you leave it with me," said Ms. Yao. "And we will see what happens. All I ask is that you keep this conversation with me confidential. Stay off social media about it. We've had enough online commotion around here for one week, haven't we?"

21 Those Who KNOW BETTER

"You actually went to see Ms. Yao?" Karin asked Jazz. "You told her Mia didn't do it?"

"I didn't say Mia was innocent," Jazz told her. "All I said was that her friends were on her phone. Most likely they were reading the post, not making it."

Karin put her arm through Jazz's. "You are the nicest person I know, Jazz Sidhu. Maybe too nice in this case. But that is why you're my best friend. You did what you thought was right. Now let's hope Mia is guilty as charged and we can move on without her in our lives."

★★★

"There's somebody here to see you."

Jazz had her earbuds in and was doing homework when her mom came into her room.

"Who?" It was strange that she would have a visitor after dinner. Any of her friends would have messaged her before coming by.

Jazz's mom had a weird look on her face. "It's Mia. She wants to talk to you."

Her mom could have said that aliens had landed on the front yard and Jazz would have been less surprised. "Mia? Why is Mia here?"

"She wants to talk to you, Jaspreet. And I said she could."

Jazz walked slowly downstairs. She could hardly believe it but, sure enough, Mia was standing in the front hall of the house.

"What do you want?" Jazz asked coldly.

"Ms. Yao told me you came to see her."

"So?" Jazz said. Her arms were folded in front of her.

"You told her it wasn't me who made that post. You said that you saw my friends playing on my phone and that it was one of them."

"I said it might have been one of them. That's all. I don't know if you did it or not. You probably did, for all I know. I know what you're like."

"You hate me," said Mia. "I guess I've given you reason to hate me. You had no reason to say anything in my defence. But you did. Why?"

"Those who know better do better." Jazz couldn't believe her mom's corny phrase came to her mouth that quickly. "I also saw what people were posting about you. It was all pretty mean. I know how it feels to be trolled like that."

Mia hung her head. "By me, you mean."

"Yes," said Jazz. "By you."

"It was those other girls who made the post," explained Mia. "My friends — my former friends anyway. They thought it was some sort of stupid joke. But the school didn't think it was funny. And none of them would admit it was them. I tried to tell Ms. Webb that I didn't do it, but no one believed me. It came from my account. And I've had some issues with that girl. We've said some things about each other in the past online. The police saw those conversations, and when you consider . . ."

". . . That you did it before? Said awful things online about me? Bullied me? Called me all sorts of names?" Jazz's voice was trembling with anger, her face flushed.

"I was really mean to you back in elementary school. I haven't been much better at Northside. My parents said I need to apologize to you. Again. But this time I mean it."

"You need to do a lot of things," said Jazz.

Mia nodded. "I need to apologize to the team and to Ms. Fridge. And I need to work on making better choices."

"Why, Mia?" asked Jazz. "Tell me why you picked on me. I never did anything to you." It was the question Jazz had been burning to ask for ages.

Mia hung her head again. "I don't know, I really don't. I guess I thought I was being funny. The people

I was friends with thought it was funny, too. I guess another thing I need to do is find better friends."

Jazz was surprised to find that, this time, she believed Mia.

Mia looked hopefully up at Jazz. "We do play pretty well together, Jazz. Maybe we could work on trying to be friends. Even as an enemy, you've been a better friend to me than those other girls."

Friends with Mia, Jazz thought. Never in a million years did Jazz imagine Mia would ask her to be friends. Jazz couldn't begin to picture it. Still, Mia had shown real concern when Jazz had turned her ankle. Jazz wanted to believe the apology Mia made was real.

"I don't know if I can do friends," said Jazz after a long silence. "Not now anyway. You hurt me a lot."

"I understand," Mia said.

"But you're right. We do play well together," Jazz added. "Maybe, just maybe, we can be real teammates instead."